Terror by Invasion

Terror by Invasion

❀

Richard D. Ondo

iUniverse, Inc.
New York Lincoln Shanghai

Terror by Invasion

Copyright © 2006 by Richard D. Ondo

All rights reserved. No part of this book may be used or reproduced by any means, graphic, electronic, or mechanical, including photocopying, recording, taping or by any information storage retrieval system without the written permission of the publisher except in the case of brief quotations embodied in critical articles and reviews.

iUniverse books may be ordered through booksellers or by contacting:

iUniverse
2021 Pine Lake Road, Suite 100
Lincoln, NE 68512
www.iuniverse.com
1-800-Authors (1-800-288-4677)

This is a work of fiction. All of the characters, names, incidents, organizations and dialogue in this novel are either the products of the author's imagination or are used fictitiously.

ISBN-13: 978-0-595-38468-6 (pbk)
ISBN-13: 978-0-595-83189-0 (cloth)
ISBN-13: 978-0-595-82849-4 (ebk)
ISBN-10: 0-595-38468-4 (pbk)
ISBN-10: 0-595-83189-3 (cloth)
ISBN-10: 0-595-82849-3 (ebk)

Printed in the United States of America

Prologue

The village of Fairport Harbor is located in northeastern Ohio. The village of Grand River is right next door. To the north, is Canada, about sixty miles away by boat or plane. These villages have small populations, 400 in Grand River and 3,300 in Fairport Harbor. Nature separates the two towns with the Grand River, which also empties into Lake Erie. Grand River is a central nerve passing through the middle of Lake County, Ohio.

Year 2000 came along without the Y2K scare that had been talked about over and over again, without any great shutdown of utilities and services. Talk about an overdone topic! The survivalists at least had their year to get ready. Someone else has been getting ready also. Terrorist cells are embedding throughout the world. This is no surprise in countries that have roots in the Middle East. Here in America, Al-Qaeda is creeping ever so slowly into small towns. Terrorism is coming in a most intriguing way. There are multiple hidden operations going on right now. Terrorist cells are using friendly bases of operation in some countries that Americans would naturally think of as allies. Second, a system of supply links feed the terrorist cells. On top of that is the country's own permissiveness, refusing to adequately protect its open borders. Illegal aliens are streaming across the southern border. A terrorist network is expanding forces around Lake Erie.

The village of Fairport Harbor has a quiet port on the southern shore of Lake Erie. The village of Grand River is a small town west of Fairport Harbor. These two towns, separated by the harbor and river, will experience an awakening of biblical proportion.

Winter on Lake Erie
The Perry Nuclear Power Plant as seen from the
Fairport Harbor Port Authority public boat ramp

East of the small boat ramps that the Fairport Harbor Port Authority has operated for years, is the Perry Nuclear Power Plant. To the west, a freighter is turning into the harbor. It will meander down the Grand River, unload the cargo it has carried, and turn around in the large basin up river. It might then pick up a load of road salt from the Road Crystal Salt Company mine, which has been in operation for decades. It goes deep underground and runs horizontally for many miles. The salt pillars left over from the mining hold up the river and portions of Lake Erie. The salt vein may extend under the two villages.

Visitors to Fairport Harbor and Grand River can slowly motor, sail, or row their boats into the harbor and traverse farther up river. Another option is to dock at the fairly new courtesy docks that the port authority maintains at the boat launch east of the river. This Lake Erie based boat launch was built with funds mostly provided by the Ohio Department of Natural Resources. This public boat launch is located next to the harbor along Lake Erie's shoreline. The boat traffic into and out of the ramp is not monitored by any specially trained people. Visitors are welcomed to these lakefront towns. The travelers coming into the harbor don't need a passport to get in. Basically, if you have money and a boat you will be able to enter freely.

That's the nature of this recreational port. Security is most lax because we haven't had trouble here since Commodore Oliver Hazard Perry battled the British on Lake Erie. That naval engagement was almost two hundred years ago.

Not much happens in this part of the world. This harbor isn't anywhere near the size of New York Harbor. The 1930s harbor security plan is quite outdated. These two villages just don't have the money for security that the county government has. These villages lack the muscle to handle a breach in security.

Richard Stern, a former member of the Fairport Harbor Port Authority Board, was always concerned about that. Richard is retired now after bowing out of public office. He saw the writing on the wall. Political life can be ruthless. He saw the political shenanigans spun by the administration and he wasn't going to get caught in that web.

The two town mayors aren't about to say anything that might draw the county commissioners into their domain. They have control of their town's operations. The overriding condition that makes this especially true is the fact that a new friend has come into their domain with a most intriguing offer. He is a rich man of Arab descent. America helped him prosper. He expresses his gratitude and joy for his success by rewarding small American towns through the use of his accumulating fortune. He is here with a plan of expansion. He envisions building a golf course, sports arena, and more. The mayors' new friend, Mr. Big, promises to make things happen. Mr. Big explains. "I will show you the money and my plan. My business team needs and demands low visibility." He adds. He has given the mayors a detailed map of a retail sports complex and park with a golf course, which would be a potent tonic to transform these two anemic towns, striving to become dignified. The two town mayors will share the limelight. They are so anxious to welcome this man.

The mayors face the problem that the river has been filling with construction silt from building projects up river. Because of this silting, the river-based marinas need dredging. They want the port authorities to secure a state grant so a dredging project can begin. The state must have matching funds to secure the grant. The marina owners are lobbying for dredging at city hall. The battle cry is, "The boaters are voters." The mayors are well aware of the boaters and the potential block of votes they stand to lose if the dredging doesn't get done. The port authorities in each town are also under fire. It is their responsibility to oversee river maintenance. They would like to help, but don't have the resources.

Mr. Big has come at the right time.

CHAPTER 1

❁

The Grand River

Today, the Grand River is a slow moving body of water about twenty to eighty yards wide. Its rather deep harbor entrance is used to handle seasonal freighter traffic.

Lake Erie and Grand River Join at the Harbor Entrance

This area is maintained by the Army Corps of Engineers. Farther up the river, the water level is much lower and not maintained. Many ships from all over the Great Lakes visit this natural harbor. Grand River is usually friendly to the boaters. Boaters travel many miles to fish and enjoy the recreational waterway. The Grand River snakes across many farmlands and around rural towns, eventually arriving at the southern shore of Lake Erie. A scenic boat ride begins right now. The river is calm today, although that isn't the case at different times of the year. History says this body of water cannot forgive those who dare manipulate her course, whether by human hands or an act of nature. This river reacts to seasonal changes. It has a personality of its own. In the winter it can freeze over. As spring approaches, the ice thaws and reacts with man's creations along the banks. Large ice flows gouge and rip apart most anything in their paths. The season is about to change now, transforming into summer.

Over the years man has changed the river's course. These changes have allowed the area's forefathers to develop great industries around the land. Father Time has removed some of these industrial plants. The land about the river's banks still bears the truth of the past—the wisdom *and* the desecration of the land, in planting these industrial sites. Buried underground, pockets of scars are forgotten by the changing civilization.

The towns of Fairport Harbor and Grand River have no roads linking each other directly. One could say that Fairport Harbor is a peninsula only one square mile inside its borders. An old railroad trestle over the river used to be the only link between the towns. That bridge has since been abandoned and torn down. All that remains are two sections with their huge pillars standing in the river. This stretch of the river is about a mile from where its mouth enters Lake Erie. It is very shallow in some areas. Beneath the shallow water are stumps, cuttings, snags, vines, and hollows. A fishing paradise it is, but it can also be a boater's nightmare. The local boater has knowledge about the river's sub terrain and knows how to traverse both up river and down.

This Grand River defines the southern end of Fairport Harbor. The beauty of this river is abundantly illustrated when one takes a boat trip from Lake Erie starting at the northern end of Fairport Harbor and goes up the river to the southern side of the village. At Fairport's harbor, where the two bodies of water meet, Lake Erie and the Grand River shake hands. Large break walls define the port and river entrance. A federal pier runs north and south out into Lake Erie. U.S. Coast Guard station is directly across the federal pier. It is one of the area's waterway rescue groups. Fairport Harbor is blessed with this fine detachment of men and women, as they maintain the only federal waterway rescue facility around this area. These coast guard folks also protect the northern U.S. border. The neighbor up north, Canada, has been an ally and a major trade partner.

On both sides of the river, mounds of stone, sand, and salt feed area blue-collar industries. A limestone company, a salt mine, and various cement works line both sides of an area immediately south of the rivers mouth. Further south, up against the flow of the river, recreational boats are exhibited on land. Some dry-docked watercraft stare at the river. Forgotten by the owners, they share land near the river's edge. A collection of sailors and fisherman, each with a Lake Erie story, inhabit the area. There's a sailboat armada tucked into an old coal-dock facility, long abandoned as industry moved away. At that sailing center, rows of massed watercraft sit, ready for adventure.

Boaters more or less know each other. They are from all walks of life. The sailing center has the adventurers, who like the challenge of the water. Another group has the prime river berthing area. This is home to the real sailors, as they surely would fess up to being. Boaters are interested in their own particular agenda. They want to enjoy that few hours on the lake and may never notice another newcomer to the area.

Lake Erie can turn mean and nasty. That's one reason this port is so important to the boaters. In the winter, boater activity is dry-docked. Some years, the Grand River will freeze over. As the winter season changes to spring, snow melts, and a new energy propagates. At this time of year, Grand River can become a torrent of iceberg paddies—thick ice flows, mighty enough to mash whatever is in their path. Fishermen and boaters have removed their docks during this time. They return in early April to see what winter damage has occurred.

Farther along, a giant basin allows lake freighter traffic to turn around. This turnaround point in the river is dredged to a depth of about twenty-seven feet. The federal government has taken charge of the river to this point. They maintain this depth out into the lake so the bigger ships can move in and out freely. The captains of these Great Lakes ships are masters at navigation. It's rare to have one of these behemoths lose control. It is to the captain's advantage to have such a straight course to traverse into the harbor. At the turning basin they can literally spin around and drive out to Lake Erie. Farther down the river there is no dredging being done by the Corps of Engineers. That is a problem for the boaters who have heavy crafts.

This South Grand River is honeycombed with small and large enterprises. Marinas, a sailing center, yacht clubs, boater associations, restaurants, and new housing developments line the next mile or so. A bouquet of restaurants adds vitality to the village of Grand River. William Tell's restaurant, the old defunct Beach Bum restaurant, Perchman's restaurant, and the Eagles Nest restaurant give class to this stretch of the river. Grand River is home to these dining extravaganzas. Being on the river's edge, they serve up meals for many boaters. Any newcomer to the area is almost sure to stop for a meal.

Mary Ann Rutherford has operated a small boat launch and dockage for many years. Boaters say she can hear a pin drop into the water. She has ample stories to tell about the river. Stop by her establishment, and you will get a full-course business lecture. She is direct, doesn't mince words, and keeps the boaters in line around her boat dock. Mary Ann and her brother John watch over the river from their vantage point.

From an island in the river, its inhabitants wave as if they are somehow immune to the forces that run with the river. Old Ram Island has endured many a confrontation with Mother Nature. Somehow that little island in the river has remained. It is almost as if Mother Nature has protected that little island from the grief of winter.

Ram Island Battered by Ice Flows

A rail bridge and Fairport Harbor's only south-exiting road bridge are along the next stretch of river. After this is an area somewhat left alone. It is peaceful on one bank and humanized on the other side. A new boat ramp is built here. This little-used area farther up river could be very valuable some day. If a visionary come calling, God only knows what potential business could develop here. A fishing club would be a good addition along this stretch. Interestingly, this area has a relatively new bridge across it. This bridge is Fairport Harbor's middle escape route into Painesville. Near here they found an old Indian burial site when they were excavating to build the new bridge. Upstream is the site of past environmental travesty. Fairport Harbor had a private dump site for village refuse. Mans past are buried here. This dump site received the usual environmental surgery required. Cover it up and it will be forgotten. Mother Nature has forgiven the residents for this abuse of the land. The Environmental Protection Agency didn't existed back when the village dump was created. Deer tracks are present and off road vehicles criss-cross the area now.

The scenic boat trip ends near an area where the river takes a sharp turn to the east. It is here that man dropped the ink bottle. Next to the river on both sides, land is slowly trying to recover from big industry droppings over the last hundred years. Again mankind turns a blind eye when industry is booming. The townsfolk preferred not to bite the hand that was feeding them. Taxes were low and employment high. Let the good times roll.

Environmental recovery work is reconditioning that spoiled land. It is a work in progress. Mother Nature is slowly nursing this area above the middle escape route back to health. Man is working to reclaim the vitality of the past, while removing the great industries of the past.

A new seed of growth is being planted. Mr. Big is coming to this area.

CHAPTER 2

❀

Meeting Night and Meet Gemini

The subject of this informal meeting is a subject that will create a commotion at city hall in Fairport Harbor. The subject of the special guest speaker is "Creating a Regional Port Authority." This would be a collection of two, three, or more county port authorities. Richard Stern could buy into this plan because most local port authorities have very little income in which to operate by themselves. Most communities don't support local port authorities. Whereas a regional port authority would have a large tax base, more political muscle, and could finance large infrastructural improvements.

The guest speaker, Mr. Columbo, speaks to favor a regional port authority, which is governed by a council of county board members. He visits from the Cleveland Port Authority. His proposal, using three area county port authorities, would have the advantage to administer large construction projects and maintain port infrastructure in each county.

Richard Stern is the only port authority representative from Fairport Harbor at this meeting. For that matter he is the only port authority board member from the entire area at this meeting. The meeting takes place in a local marina. The local boaters are starting to ask questions, "Hey Richard, why isn't your other board member here for this meeting?" Richard couldn't bring himself to tell them that they wouldn't be interested in county control. "Our board members are tied up this evening and I'm here as a representative." Richard shamefully dodged the truth. Richard admitted to himself, "Well, this port authority issue that Mr. Columbo is talking about is sacred ground for a good many politicians."

Suddenly, Richard had a vision. His mind transmitted an unusual thought. "Mr. Columbo is not what everyone thinks. He's here for another reason." Richard listened to the speech given by this gentleman. He spoke with an accent. He had a dark complexion, with sunken eyes. He was well groomed with a graying, short-cropped beard. His business suit, a gray pinstripe, looked to be top of the line. Richard drew a mental picture of this person's political culture in his mind. A negative thought crossed Richard's mind. "This person is one of them. A cold chill ran down his body. They are inside our Cleveland port system." Richard couldn't bring himself to say, "The terrorists are here."

Mr. Columbo had a bracelet on his right wrist. A lion symbol was inscribed on it. A large scar was visible under his right eye. Richard shook his head as if to clear the evil thought, "This can't be." Richard still had the smell of beer on his breath and he thought the beer must be affecting his thought process. He silently said, "I wish I hadn't stopped at the social club before I came here."

All attendees were moved by his speech. They were riveted to their seats and gave him a standing ovation when he finished talking. During his speech he gave some financial reasons to become a county port authority. He never spoke about the security issues that Richard was expecting to hear. Richard expected at least a rudimentary statement about port security measures enacted after 9/11.

The audience asked, "Would the regional port authority include Lake County?" The speaker, Mr. Columbo said, "We could join hands with your county port authority." Richard thought to himself, "No way will it work here. The mayors will crush this idea."

Richard could hear it now, the first word out of the mayor's mouth, "*No-No-No.*" Richard says under his breath, "Why not? It is because this is mayoral sacred ground. Also, we would be treading on the territory of some well-established port authority boards. The mayors appoint members to these bodies and they don't want to lose that right."

Richard's suggestion is to have a Lake County Port Authority for the expressed reason of port security by county deputy sheriffs. A greater regional port authority would be formed for financial leverage. The county and regional port authorities would coexist. Richard's idea will bring down the house like Hurricane Katrina. Richard is going to be alone in this matter. It will be a reason that he finally gives up being a port authority board member. Even though he still is in the fight, he doesn't have any backers. It is time for him to stop beating his head against the wall. Richard refuses to give it up.

Richard is a Gemini. He sometimes thinks two people are living inside his body. Richard is one of the two personalities. He has this supernatural sense to look into the past and the future through his dreams. It is not completely plain to understand these dreams as they come in fits and starts. This is especially true if he's under the influence of alcohol. Richard is vague and indecisive. Often he is confused because of his repeated use of alcohol. He's tried a number of times to gain control of his alcoholic disease. Rick, the other personality, comes to life and acts on the dreams. Rick is like an umpire making a snap decision when reading these signs inside Richard's dreams. Rick hopes to prevent a major terrorist act by developing this mental imperfection. The two personalities are both competing and complementing each other. Rick and Richard, the Gemini twins, are locked in one body. One of them is dominant.

Richard first realized the mystery of his dreams at the informational meeting with guest speaker Mr. Columbo. He wasn't totally sure what message the dreams were telling him, but he sort of concluded that he was seeing clues to his dreams. His dreams enlighten Rick. Rick is determined to know what other dreams are locked within Richard. Richard is an alcoholic under construction. He hasn't become totally oblivious to living. Richard has told social workers that he sometimes will have flashbacks and sees some unusually graphic details. He has seen weird graphics of the past entering into the present. The social workers explain that these experiences are tied to alcohol abuse. Richard knows he is both addicted and allergic to booze. The problem is he hasn't yet released his love of the unending spiral of alcoholism. Rick seems to step in and sober Richard up. Rick won't do that until he has answers to Richard's dreams. Richard still likes to beat himself up by abusing alcohol. He cannot understand this senseless journey with alcohol and his supernatural experience. He needs to somehow connect to his mind and this problem. He may escape from this nightmare in his life. He is drawn to God for hope and prays for a great revelation.

CHAPTER 3

❀

Bin Laden Directive

Osama Bin Laden's directives are sent out by foot soldiers. It is a slow process but the possibility of an intercept is reduced. His notes explain in a pressing manner, "It is imperative our fighting equipment be slipped into Canada at a rigorous pace. The safe houses that are secure could become compromised because of enemy infiltration. Our buildup must quicken. Canadian cells are becoming exposed and it will be harder to use Canada as a source of our invasion of America."

The terrorists are amassing the war machine in pieces, bit by bit, and transferring most of them to the Canadian border. A marina and repair shop is effectively used to aid in the disbursement. Some of the packaging material is bought in Canada. The process of assembly is done at a Lake Erie marina. The final inspection must be done in America. Store cells that are planted in America will handle delivery of the equipment. When the battle plan is executed, supercell leaders will use their stores to arm the cell members. That moment is fast approaching.

In America, the terrorists have for years bought into the food service businesses. The food stores are providing a home base. The stores are a source of money and a place for the cells to glow. They have been disciplined in planning this part of an attack. Each year the planted operatives learn more about how to function in their role.

Bin Laden's men received enough flight training in American schools to score a home run and embolden the terrorists. The success of 9/11 actually caused some disruption in his long range plan. America became more aggressive, putting terrorist activities on the defensive. In the stores themselves, customers stopped buying from the planted operatives because people recognized their facial features. If customers suspected a store is owned by an Arab business person, those stores were boycotted. The stores owned by Middle-Eastern men were also singled out. When this happened, some of Bin Laden's donors, people of Arab descent, lost some stores when payments couldn't be made. A ripple effect took place. The charity operatives were being squeezed, which caused capital to dry up. Supercell leaders, who operate stores, now operate in a more clandestine way. It was obvious that store owners needed to change their appearance. Owners are hiring unsuspecting young Americans as low-level associates. They are hired to cast an appearance of an American owned store. This plan will hide the pretension of a stores ownership. Store owners had their Arab women change their appearance to reflect an American style.

Fortunately for Bin Laden, Canada is still friendly to most Arabs. Canada is safe for now. Bin Laden thinks about past events. His British Al-Qaeda cell moved too quickly when they caused the subway attack in England. This attack strengthened his enemy's watch over there. The British suffered a blow from his cell, but this made the Canadians take notice. That was a mistake made in timing. About the same time, a senior Pakistani cell member was arrested in Pakistan. Computer records were found. This important data caused more cell members to be arrested. This breakup brought Bin Laden to his present state of affairs. He says, "We must bring our experts into the USA and quickly put an attack into motion." He didn't envision moving ahead with an American invasion until 2009 or 2010, but now says, "We cannot wait another year. Our momentum is slipping. Certain world events are forcing us to commit to the early attack.

"We have roots well established throughout the world. Now, with the natural disasters in the United States, America is off guard. Their balance is slipping because of hurricanes. These natural disasters are sending us a signal. All events are weighed in and considered. Bin Laden feels time is right. We have held our fire long enough. They will lose hope if we are successful in a new attack. By striking in a small American town or two, a wave of public doubt about terrorism will sweep across America. Americans will realize they can't be safe from attack. A mission like this will increase our ability to influence lesser nations. Al-Qaeda will be honored for their heroic mission. We will make an entire country's economy weak. This work will help shift the war back in our favor. Third world nations will align themselves with our programs if we score a victory. The current administration will suffer at the opinion polls. The politicians in America will waffle. That will help our cause as they blame each other."

The council of elders sits with Osama Bin Laden. After a lengthy discussion, they make the case that waiting any longer will only place the invasion in jeopardy. Bin Laden raises his rifle and recites a passage from the Quran. "Islamic teaching shall be spread throughout the world. That is our goal.

"Weakness in American border security creates a golden opportunity for us. American troops will pull back from their foreign bases when we attack them in their own country. They will try to shore up their borders, and we will have a free reign to stoke the fire of Islam in other countries." He is confident in his speech.

Bin Laden talks about the reality of the war. "The Iraq war has cost us valuable members. A number of our best fighters have died at the hands of the infidels. Some countries have reduced their role in helping our cause. Any wave of democratic governing is a cancer to our cause.

"Many of our European soldiers have been pooled together and sent to Iraq via Syria. We need these border countries like Syria and Iran to act as infiltration routes. In the last six months we have suffered some serious losses at the border of Iraq and Syria. United States marine and army forces cut our supply lines. Iraqi forces are working with the infidels in greater numbers. That act is helping the enemy secure public confidence. Security and communications are becoming increasingly problematic. We don't have the training camps in place in Iraq that we once had. Recruits from Europe are not getting the training needed. Another disturbing action has been with both France and Germany. They are handcuffing training centers. The major mosques in these countries are under investigation. The combination of all these actions gives credence to the next step that we must take. I have sent the orders out using foot soldiers, Arabian News, and Al Jazeera. The Internet is helping with our supply codes. Supercell leaders will decode messages using arranged stores. Attack northern Ohio, that is our next target," Bin Laden commands. "We must hold together," he pleads.

The person most responsible for many terrorist operations around the world is Osama Bin Laden. He is the number one terrorist and the ringleader of Al-Qaeda. Sometimes spelled Al-Quida, this organization is a breeding ground for terrorists. Bin Laden still works a terror campaign using the media but is clearly hidden from physical view. He puts out video and audiotapes for the news media. By doing this, he is sending a message to the planted cells. He calls for another campaign in America.

Bin Laden is doing a balancing act with his forces. He professes to his circle of confidants. "Great care must be taken now. Some of our brothers have been taken down in the struggle to free the world of the Western menace. The West has managed to upset our game of terror and fear. America and Pakistan have shaken our religious chess board that we carefully orchestrated. The Saudi government is frustrating our workers there. Our training grounds are drying up. Some cells that are sitting in the world's weaker nations continue to be harried by undercover agents and military pressure. We have been moved about the world reducing our chances to coordinate an attack. I liken this to the cat fleeing from the dog. We could call some nations home but that is being increasingly hampered by the new West. The old American regime is gone, replaced by a more determined crusader. His armies are committed to beat down our insurgency, city by city, in Iraq. With this taking place, our religious war against Israel is hampered. Resources are devoted to the Iraqi theater, which reduces our efforts in other lands. It was easier to operate when the other American president was in office. The new American leadership has forced us to change our tactics. The difficulties in Afghanistan shifted our base of operation."

By now Bin Laden is mad. He erupts. "This is why I'm living in a remote camp!" He goes on, "It is not so easy to stay ahead of the enemy's military nowadays. Our hope at winning is resting on the cells already in place. They may break the American people's appetite for war." Osama Bin Laden continues, "We must send word to the super cells in America. Today the suicide experience is used in Israel and Iraq. Tomorrow it will be coming to America."

CHAPTER 4

Meet Some Players

I arrived at a Monday night port authority meeting as I usually do. Not a big deal and it didn't seem that this meeting was going to be any different than the others.

I was the chairman. At fifty years old I had been in many battles. My alcoholism is in remission for now, if you want to say going without for a couple days is remission. I am a divorced father of three children. I'm not afraid to speak the truth as I see it. What is politically incorrect will cost me my board chairmanship.

The port authority old guard was a group that only did enough to continue to line their pockets with monthly salary. This being the case, a couple old guard board members still remain. They operate with caution. They regard me as "the loose cannon." I will eventually be demoted to vice chairman, so I won't make the newspapers. You see, we have a big ego trip going on in the mayor's quarters and the port authority has been stealing the show this year. This is riding high on the mayor. He is becoming second fiddle.

I was one of two board members agreeing to go to a meeting with South Grand River Marina folks. Seems that the water level is low in the river and the marina boaters are concerned about getting their boats out to Lake Erie this season. The marinas in the area are experiencing rather low water levels at their sites because Lake Erie's water level is low. They need port authority intervention to seek governmental help with dredging. A request for a dredging permit is applied for and approved after considerable debate. A permit is issued from the Army Corps of Engineers. Now somebody has to come up with the money to pay for the dredging. This port authority never had much to do with the South Grand River.

I'm sitting among four other board members and one female secretary, Brenda Clark. These folks are from various walks of life. The current port authority board is a mixture of people with fresh ideas, an improved batch. Each member has created a niche in life for himself. They are not professionals in the sense that they are only dedicated to the port authority. Some have day jobs and can hardly be called upon to get together at a moment's notice. Right now, this assembly is made up of retired workers and the actively employed. The port authority board has some well-intended ideas.

The mayor confides in port authority board member number two, who is the godfather and treasurer of the port authority. Salvador Cambello is dominant, commanding, and manipulative at times. By controlling the finances, he handcuffs the port authority. Being a retired railroad investigator, he often comes on strong. He has a way of getting under everyone's skin. The port authority board has lost board members and workers who just can't deal with the godfather. Many citizens privately acknowledge that the godfather is not to be trusted. He has his own agenda. People, who are close to him, sometimes find him abrasive and pushy. Cloaked under the great-community-service image are the feisty, peppery attitude and a control freak. He is a cigar smoker, with a football player's stature. He can muddy the waters and will foot drag until he gets his way. The chairman has found out if he challenges him and is persistent long enough, he will end up folding his tent and running for cover. Our third board member is the current vice chairman and next puppet chairman. Mason Renolds is meshed into a number of small enterprises. His racing cars have earned him fame and fortune. He inherited a flower shop. He and his retired brother stand to inherit a substantial real-estate fortune. He is an avid runner, a marathon man. He has been a member of the board for many years. He is seasoned and has a knack for being in on "deals that will turn a few bucks." His long ramblings on topics are very disturbing to other board members, who often whisper under their breath, "*Oh no*, lots of long wind coming, Mason is talking. Be prepared for a long speech."

Our newly appointed, final two board members were each picked by the mayor, one recommended to the mayor by the godfather and the other a friend of the chairman. The godfather wants Victor Tomlinson because they are both retired and they play handball together. He'll be a "yes man" for the godfather, rubber-stamping whatever the godfather says.

Our last board member is a youngster at twenty-one years old. Seth Wood has a job with the village and is at the mercy of the mayor. Newly married, he must be careful in his deliberations to not run out of line with the mayor's ideas. He has a good work ethic and can interact well with the board. His appointment being so new gives him enough distance from making decisions. He can just go along with the other board members. Seth is far removed from the big picture. His appointment will be short, as the godfather will do unto him as he has to others. The godfather will lean on him until he becomes fed up and resigns.

This board should be acting independently. It can't do that because of the tampering from the mayors' offices. The same is true of the Grand River Port Authority. The mayors just have to control. They select the right person for "their" job. They want someone who thinks the "right" way, someone who can go along with the mayors' agenda. It is said that a port authority has the same power as a village council. It *should* be free to explore and improve conditions about this Grand River and Fairport Harbor area. Laws mandate the port authority to oversee improvements and maintain infrastructure that affect our harbor. Well now, how can the mayors and the port authority cause an apocalypse? Richard could see inside a devious plan being hatched by the cunning mayor and his cohorts. A never ending dredging tax will be imposed on the boaters. The port authority must approve to make this happen. The mayors were not afraid to command the port authorities to seek a tax on the boaters. This way they are sheltered from criticism for enacting an unfavorable tax.

At a meeting the port authority board brings with them a collection of ideas about the tax. The Mayor Conway suggests, "We need to change the name from *tax* to *river or dock fee*." After receiving mayoral advice, a harbor *user fee* is agreed upon. "This will capture all the boaters up river that use the harbor," says Sal Cambello. Sal rubs his hands together as if he's preparing for a feast.

How the board members vote is subject to mayoral pressure. As usual, the board members side with the mayor. You see, the mayor appoints all board members. Such is the case on both sides of the river. This nasty political abuse of power leads these two towns down a dangerous path. Mayor Conway won his battle on the user fee issue but Grant Michell didn't pass muster. Grand River boaters shot him down. That killed the user fee idea.

Our two village mayors are basic followers of the rule that says be at the right place at the right time and good things should happen. Miss that opportunity and bad can happen. Our mayor from Grand River, Grant Michell, controls a small town of middle-class citizens. He's a good man. His sister, Bonnie

Michell Gray, is a real estate developer of a large town to the south. Because that town is making great strides in development, our small-town mayor needs to create something. He's not one to miss an opportunity when he sees it. This is where he and the Fairport Harbor mayor run together. They both are opportunists, bathed in politics. They are control freaks. The Fairport Harbor mayor, Reese Conway, is well accustomed to the financial world. He strung together an impressive number of wins in the stock market when most investors were heading for cover. He controls a number of money accounts at his primary job. Being a bank president has helped get him into the political arena. His bank contributed to the Columbus gubernatorial race. This provided him a political foothold in Columbus. Endorsement from area politician helped in his mayoral race. It was no coincidence that this mayor was elected at a time when Fairport Harbor residents were searching for someone who wasn't creating a commotion at village hall. The new mayor is trim and polished. He is a college guy who is very likable.

Low and behold it's Reese to the rescue. He married into a political background. His ex-wife's father was a Columbus mayor. That girl saw something in Reese. They married, and years later, after he became mayor, she divorced him. Gossip in Fairport Harbor permeates most dining rooms. People saw the writing on the wall as Reese was always around high rollers. A good many of the social butterflies were ladies. We do know that Reese Conway is a ladies' man. He frequents high buck private card clubs. Private golf courses and racetracks are a couple more places you might find him. Then again he plays big stakes card games every once in a while so Los Vegas is certainly on his vacation list. He likes the limelight.

Richard sat silently contemplating his next move. The port authority board members were called together by the mayor to review a problem. Richard had made remarks to the newspapers and he sent a letter to the Lake County commissioners detailing reasons to institute a county port authority and forming a regional port authority. He told the newspaper reporter his personal views, "The port authorities in Fairport Harbor and Grand River Village need to free themselves from local administrative influence and become closer to the county administration." That very notion caused a furor within Fairport's mayoral hierarchy. The mayor is not about to relinquish authority to the county. He could sense that fellow members of the port authority board were also ruffled, as Richard sat with them at this special meeting called by the mayor. The mayor needed to get some answers about Richard's remark to the newspaper. Richard was on display. He felt like he was on the stage of a Broadway play. Bonnie Clark, the secretary, seemed to be his only friend. She keeps herself far removed from politics. She is smart enough to simply watch the action from the sidelines. Everyone else had a stone face. Their lips would have fractured if they smiled.

In another room, arguing voices are heard. Mayor Conway is mad. The newspapers are writing articles about letters that Mr. Stern sent to county commissioners. These letters are causing major county players to look into a Lake County port authority. In private consultation, the mayor and his legal advisor discuss a way to remove Chairman Stern. He has to get rid of that current chairman. Stern's ideas are stealing the show. Behind the scene, the mayor build's a plan to install Mason Renolds as chairman. Mason will eventually unseat Richard because of Richard's personal comments to the newspapers and the commissioners. Mayor Conway can't get rid of Richard so easily because that would be interfering in another branch of government. The mayor would have to wait two years until Richard Stern's appointment runs out and not reappoint him to the board.

"That will take too long," says the mayor. They can refute Stern's remarks by writing a rebuttal letter to the county commissioners and the newspaper and regain an upper hand. Since Stern's reappointment is not up for two more years, moving him down to vice chairman will put Mayor Conway back on center stage. A demotion of Stern will make it look as if Stern is out of touch with his fellow board members.

Mayor Conway devises his plan. He'll make a phone call to the right person. "Hello, Sal, this is a friend of Mayor Conway." The mayor disguises his voice as he talks. "I heard the mayor express a need for a vote of confidence against the port authority chairman. It seems like city hall administration thinks Mason should be the chairman. Do you get the message?" The anonymous caller abruptly hangs up. Naturally, the caller ID registers as "unknown caller." Salvador Cambello says, "That's a good idea."

Days later, the monthly meeting of the port authority convenes. The godfather is prepared to help the mayor. Sal requests to have a vote of confidence in the service that the chair is providing.

Behind the scenes, the mayor watches his steps unfold to advance his secret advice of switching the vice chairman and chairman. Reacting on the anonymous caller's suggestion, Salvador Cambello moves that a vote of NO-confidence be taken of the board members to see if they can work with the chair because of the personal letter to the county commissioners. A no-confidence vote is taken. Each board member recommends a change is needed. The godfather leads off with a fiery litany. Mr. Renolds follows. This is all bad news for Richard. Victor reinforces Cambello's statements. Only Seth Wood would hesitate on this one, but decides to go along with the other board members. Richard faithfully follows with his resignation of the chairman's seat. He gives way to Mason Renolds. At the next port authority meeting, Mason Renolds gets the nod to take over the chairmanship. The port authority becomes politically correct and in line with what the mayor says. The port authority board is now at the mercy of Mason, the pontificator. What happen here is twofold. The headline grabber, Richard, is put on the back burner. The county commissioners receive a letter from the port authority indicating Chairman Stern has been demoted. Since Richard Stern was the one who asked the county commissioners to examine the possibility of converting the local port authority into a county port authority, his credibility is sunk by his demotion. The county commissioner can delete his idea from their agenda. The county commissioners see Stern as someone who is out of step with his peers. The port authority appointments will be kept in the mayor's hands. The mayor can rest easy. The public didn't have a reaction to what was going on because port authority operations are very low on the public's radar screen. Richard's self-confidence sinks. He returns to the bottle.

Richard will soon resign after this embarrassing demotion. Richard admits to himself that he's been too forward with his ideas. He'll move out of the way and yield to the old guard. He can campaign about the terrorist threat by writing to his congressmen and talking to the local folk.

Richard is now released from most official business. He will feed his habit. He stops more often at the local taverns and clubs. They become a retreat. He is despondent and disconnected from most public affairs. He refuses to get help with his addiction to alcohol. He keeps having wild dreams after his drinking sessions in the bars. He's in denial with his drinking and depression. While not often, he loses focus on the time of day and the days of the week. His promotional work suffers but he pushes on. He makes extra money under the table by photographing sports events.

Richard would still like the county to oversee the administering of the harbor and port. He knows the terrorist threat is out there. It is waiting. The bigger county control will bring in a source of new revenue and provide better harbor protection for the towns. Their police force would be more capable of handling a terrorist threat than the two small communities could provide. He's more concerned then ever about the possibility that our waterway could become host to a potential terrorist threat. His concern is a sneak attack. He believes the attack is eminent from the north. His gut feeling and the strange dreams of terror are his reasons.

One evening, after consuming a number of sixteen-ounce longnecks, Richard goes into a deep sleep. Rick appears in this dream. *Rick sees something. A vision appears of a lion that jumps from boat to boat ravaging the passengers. The party boats are from Canada. He sees the maple leaf emblem on the side of the boats.* The dream ends as the phone rings. "Hello, I say hello." Richard hears a political message about supporting the mental health levy. He says, "Yeah, right, good bye." He clicks the phone down on the receiver. He's a little disappointed that he woke up because he saw his Gemini twin in the dream. "Rick gives me a sense of trust," he says. Richard decides to put the bottle down for a couple days to get focused. He's starting to understand himself. Confusion seems to abate when he thinks of himself as Rick. He doesn't exactly understand why he has these mood swings. He decides to talk to Father Pete. The Catholic priest has been a pillar of understanding and guidance in the community.

It was a confessional conference. Father Pete did understand, as I knew he would. He offered some timely suggestions and told me of treatment programs for people who become overwhelmed by alcohol, drugs, etc. I was somewhat ready to accept his advice, but not ready enough. I still wanted to explore the mystery of my dreams.

I went back home and sat there. I knew Father Pete was right but I walked over to the refrigerator and pulled out a cold one. I downed one and then another. I started to recall the past events by daydreaming.

A rub against losing local control of the port authorities is that the community doesn't have a say in what happens at the boat ramp. They might lose that control under county management. Most citizens in Fairport Harbor don't care one way or another. The town folks could benefit with lower taxes and better service by having county control. However, the board members of Fairport's port authority run the risk of losing the $200 bucks a month board member pay. I will lose this battle four to one because of my being in favor of county control. It is out of the question with the mayor, and the mayor is not about to surrender control of those port authority board appointments he gets to make. For sure the godfather is equally afraid of losing his power. The godfather does even better. He earns $300 bucks a month because he controls the treasurer's job.

The port authority board is about to be called into the back room, that is also called the Executive Chamber, for an exclusive meeting with the mayor and his legal advisor.

The board members can hear into the back room, from their vantage point. It's obvious the mayor and his legal counsel need to move swiftly and get Richard Stern out of the papers. They both favor a full sacking and removal but fear political backlash. Richard has been instrumental in getting money into Fairport's harbor and recreation system. His teaming up with the Corp of Engineers and the Ohio Department of Watercraft has been most beneficial for Fairport Harbor. Without his push, projects stall and get forgotten.

The mayor calls the board into the Executive Chamber. The mayor, his lawyer, and the port authority board listen as the mayor outlines his concern with Richard. All agree with the mayor and each person systematically blasts Richard for a letter sent to the county commissioners.

Mason and Salvador find that Richard has to often gone to marina meetings without board approval. While they may be by personal invitation, he has acted as a board member on official duty. When he speaks at these meetings, it appears that his personal view is a majority point of view of the board.

The mayor's counsel takes his turn. The attorney blasts off, "What the F is going on here, Stern. You are not part of the team. We have to straighten this letter's information out that you sent to the commissioners." The attorney adds, "We'll construct a retractors letter to counter this letter by Chairman Richard."

I knock over the beer on the table as I snap out of my daydream. The can was almost empty. I wipe up the minor spill and grab one more. "This will be my last one," I say. I can see I still have three more cans in the fridge. I sit again and start thinking again.

Why request the county be more involved in the politics and mechanisms used to operate a port? I believe the mayor and the port authority board is missing a golden opportunity to tap into county funds for future security and expansion. Certainly the county would be better equipped to foresee and handle most pending harbor problems. I can't tell the mayor I had a vision of the future after a beer-drinking-induced dream. I know the terrorist problem is real. It could arrive at our border. It is not anything the mayor and his men would want to hear about at this time. The mayors are more concerned about a tax on boaters that they can sneak into law if they can keep the county commissioners out of the way. I believe the two mayors have concocted a plan together. They will pass a tax on the boaters for harbor maintenance. Their never-ending tax will fill the town's general fund at the expense of the local boaters. The tax is disguised as a river dredging fund for future use.

"I'm going to have one more," I say as I break out of my thoughts. "There's only two more left. I'll be making a pit stop tomorrow. I'm always talking to myself. I believe my guardian angel is around me. At least she will listen to me."

The only person against this ailing tax scheme is Richard. He knows the county is much better prepared for collecting such a tax. County control would ensure the money would end up getting a better bang for any dollars collected. He also believes that a tax by the county would be small compared to what the mayors have dreamed up. Finally, in the end, the businesses along the river smell the plot themselves and kill the river tax.

The mayors will not be outwitted. They have additional ways to lead. There is simply too much at stake. The boaters will need to ante up their own money when the tax issue goes down to defeat. The political mischief will fester as greed, jealousy, and a thirst for more power takes hold of sane men.

The boaters started to point a finger at the mayors for using the port authority to push a dredging tax through. The mayors now have a stain on their political shirts. The boaters are wise to these two rascals. The two mayors almost got away with it. However, they will still use the port authority plan for dredging.

Richard convinces area boaters to support a voluntary donation to raise money for dredging. He asks the federal and state officials to help fund and oversee the dredging of the river. The port authority board comes together and finds a solution to fund the project. The dredging does get done.

There was another motive driving the mayors to seek a tax. A new found friend is about to enter the scene. Someone with big bucks is coming into the area. Great promises are heaped upon the shoulders of the political bosses. The two towns may share in the rewards of someone who is a partner with the devil.

CHAPTER 5

❀

The Letter

I stopped at village hall to pick up a free beach sticker so I could park my car at the beach parking lot during the summer. Once a year for a week this parking lot is closed. Fairport Harbor is host to a big Independence Day Mardi Gras that attracts thousands of festival revelers. They close this parking lot down so merchants can erect their tents in an oval shape throughout the parking area. Everyone has to park on top of the hill inside the village and walk down to the Mardi Gras.

While I was at village hall I inquired about opening a new business in Fairport Harbor. The village administrator, Horst Beamer, invited me into his office to explain the details. "I just got off the phone with the mayor. It's business as usual around here. Of course, you know this town, nothing happens around here," he said.

He had a registration form that needed to be filled out by a new business owner, like me, but it was his last copy. He asked me to wait in his office while he went downstairs to get more forms from the secretary. I was standing by his desk and noticed a letter addressed to the mayor. I walked around the desk to check out this letter. While I felt uneasy about being so inquisitive, I absolved myself by saying to myself, "This is a public place. If he didn't want me to see the letter, he would have put it away." I started to read the letter and my eyes started to water as I forced myself to speed read. I focused on the scoop I was reading. It appeared the mayor hit the jackpot. For every thousand bucks Fairport came up with, a certain gentleman would add one million dollars to the local economy. I did some fast reading and had to turn the page. This information made me feel a little guilty. I flipped the paper back to its original place.

Beamer came back into the room with a number of fresh copies. He handed me one and wished me good luck. Horst Beamer reminded me of a German Field Marshall, like Rommel in Hitler's army. He had round glasses, and I could picture him in a military uniform. I watched him place a book over the letter as if he knew he slipped up. "Have a good day general, I mean Horst." I said absent-mindedly. With that, I made a fast exit.

"I'm going to keep my mouth shut." I said to myself. "Old gossip town Fairport Harbor would be buzzing if they heard of this news." I decided to drive over to the club and reward myself for a fine investigative job. I felt like I had achieved a small victory.

The two town mayors received identical letters announcing the arrival of a maverick developer.

Honorable Mayors of Fairport Harbor and Grand River you are about to be rewarded for your dedication and hard work. Your communities have been singled out by a select group of specialists that recognize areas of potential. Feel extremely distinguished that your towns were selected among the hundreds of U.S. communities fitting a narrow research criterion. This letter professes a passion for helping small communities overcome slow growth by furnishing capital through a special overseas fund. Using your excellent management skills and your 1/1000 matching contribution, fantastic growth will be at your disposal.

A powerful oil magnet established this account in gratitude for his successful business ventures. He was made a very rich man because of America's commitment in helping small third-world countries from which he came. His forefathers left him a substantial fortune. He wishes he could help improve and give back to America in some way. His ideal approach is to lend money to small American communities.

He actually buys his way into small communities and sets up enterprises such as convenience stores, retail and sports shops, and recreational facilities from which to operate. These small businesses will go on to flourish and be left with the communities after the seeds of success are sown. A small dividend is paid back by the businesses, and over the years everyone is rewarded. This man of wealth will bring to the mayor's town great promise of prosperity and high property value.

You, dear mayors, will be made main leaders to showcase this plan. We are looking for additional waterway property to build a recreational center and reli-

gious foundation. Natural gas projects in the area make land surrounding Grand River and Fairport Harbor a natural location. We know that you can easily annex property for the good of your communities. With this being noted, I am sure you will be willing to take the necessary steps to acquire land as indicated.

The land mentioned in the letter is down the river and a possible target to be recovered from its past uses and/or abuses. A federal environmental superfund project has been devoted to restoring land around the area.

Mayor Grant Michell of Grand River and Mayor Reese Conway are just beside themselves. It's as if they have hit the lottery. Because of their egos and the letter's contents, the facts of the letter remain secret to all but the mayor's administrator.

This private letter points out that projects such as theirs could become troubled if any information were to leak out.

Your river and outlet to the lake is of special interest. In this regard, noble mayors, we ask that you withhold information about this endeavor. Strict confidentiality is essential. We are committing vast resources in money and labor. You will see a determined effort to make your community a Mecca of luxury living.

Since both mayors are aware of each other's grasp of politics, they set in motion a plan to really capitalize on this newly found opportunity. Blinded by their own personal emotions they calculate how far up the political ladder this could take them. Each mayor has dreams of greatness. Why? A possible Ohio representative seat could be gained here.

I found out a piece of the mayors plan for exacting a tax from the boaters because of my position as chairman with the port authority. It came from a usually tight-lipped source. I was talking to Horst Beamer when he was a little drunk in the bowling alley bar. He said, "The port authority has to assume some money will go into the general fund." It was something like that but I was under the influence also. I did not like what was going on as the two mayors' manipulated wording in a document to conceal the fact that money for a dredging project would end up being a general revenue fund for the villages to use after the dredging was complete. Their plan to tax the boaters was a never-ending tax.

Richard had already convinced the boaters to send money to the port authority treasurer. That was a struggle, but after many meetings he convinced the boaters they would have to share in the cost of dredging. The boaters finally agreed to a one-time voluntary commitment.

The mayors could skim some money from the dredging fund set up by the boaters for dredging if they could get their tax plan approved. The money that was being collected by the port authority treasurer, Salvador Cambello, could be used by the villages to help fund a new secret project. The mayors would promise to repay the money Sal Cambello would lend them. If the money issues surfaced, the port authorities would take the heat.

If all goes well, the mayors will soak up political kudos derived from their newfound opportunity. They meet each other at a small diner to discuss their plans. The place is well away from their towns. They agreed that it is imperative that they keep all knowledge about the plans only to close administrators. They also agreed that the wealthy investor must be kept secret. They have a big-time developer coming into town and he is going to stimulate the village's bankroll. It is too good to be true. Mayor Michell, the conservative Grand River mayor, is a little apprehensive. Conway can see the strain in his face. "Don't get cold feet on me, Grant." Mayor Conway does his best to convince Michell.

Mayor Conway has dealt with many high buck deals over the years. He can't pass on an opportunity of this magnitude. A token investment will turn these two villages into money machines. For small pocket change and some flexible political maneuvering, great things can happen. Reese explains, "Listen Grant, you're about to become a legend. We have the port authority working the river project. We are using their money. There will be plenty of money in that account. Money can be maneuvered in and out of that account. Nobody is going to notice. I have Sal where I need him. He won't mind a little shifting if he gets something. What we do is help our communities by using a little fiscal money management. I'll work with Sal. He's up for reappointment if you know what I mean." The two mayors stare at each other and each realizes they have done this before.

Later, the mayor meets with Cambello. "Sal, I really want you to retain your position on the port authority board. You'll need to work with me on a financial matter." The political vise is applied to leverage a favor. Salvador Cambello, the godfather, would hate to lose his title and the seat on the port authority board. "Don't worry, mayor," says Sal. A large grin creases his face.

Mr. Big needs to have local control of development, which our two mayors will supply. Mr. Big has deep pockets. He can make things happen if he can sway local politicians into approving his plan. He will make some adjustments to the river and its surrounding lands. By using the mayor's influence with the port authority he'll be able to do the project. The mayors know they will need a source of revenue to help with Mr. Big's lofty plans. The letter indicated a need for some in-kind service. This is a small price to pay for the big bucks about to flow into these two villages. Sometimes a small tale needs to be told to exact a monetary measure. Both mayors have surmised the eventual passage of an emergency river-dredging tax. They don't give up on the tax issue. They will craft a special message to their councils and try again with the tax idea. Without going into much detail the message will explain a need to deepen the river. Boater safety is at risk. The port authority supports this message as they have been in close contact with area marinas. This special dredging tax will supply both mayors and their hidden agenda with an operations fund. Reese has another ace in his hand if the second dredging tax should fail. He can call upon Sal for more liquidity. This is so clever a way to disguise the real plans for the money. Reese will invest in Mr. Big's plan and all the money is spent under the pretext of river maintenance. His timing is impeccable. The boaters need help. The port authority is applying for a dredging grant, and the town mayors, are here to help both.

The town mayors and the entrepreneur need to forge a union of trust to operate a successful business venture. The mayors are busy cutting deals for land acquisition. The opening of a new boat ramp is needed and a permit to operate is quickly signed. These small victories are accomplished in record time. Mr. Big brings in workers almost miraculously. He uses his knowledge of illegal alien activity to pool his manpower. Much of this action is moved along at breakneck speed. It is those proverbial cash envelopes that Mr. Big's lieutenants provide; bribes make the difference when issues need to be overcome.

With Mr. Big, the mayors will come out smelling like fine cologne. They will see to it that Mr. Big gets his plans approved. Behind the scene, the mayors talk to each other over lunch and dinner. They meet a couple times each week to format the plan. They build a confidence by sharing in each others' public experiences. Grant has a better grasp of public office. Reese is a master of leveraging money.

People who have money turn to Reese Conway to build their fortune. As one citizen remarks, "The mayor steps on a dollar, and it turns into five bucks." He has transformed the town. The same is happening in Grand River village. Grant's coolness under fire makes him a trustworthy neighbor. Both mayors only release enough information about the building project going forward along the river to keep the public off the real trail. All of these things came about when the developer arrived.

CHAPTER 6

The Developer Arrives

Mr. Big is a Middle-Eastern oil sheik who has wealthy relatives living around the Persian Gulf. He is middle-aged. A tall man with graying long hair and a short, groomed beard, he sticks out in a crowd because of his stature. His build suggests he's been in a few fights. He has a scar on the bridge of his nose and scars on both cheeks. People working for Mr. Big have learned not to question his judgments, as he fires and hires without much discussion. His core family of three chief lieutenants and two legal advisors surround him. Their task is to keep the inquisitive public away.

Mr. Big's counsel gives advice to the mayors. "Honorable mayors, we have come to the village hall in Fairport Harbor to personally present a generous offer from our leader. Mr. Big is here for your scrutiny. He is very skillful in leading untapped potential to the door of opportunity. Towns that have been stuck in neutral, shift gears when Mr. Big lends a helping hand. Your turn has arrived. Spend a little of your valuable time witnessing an offer you may never receive again. Mr. Big will plant a seed here, between these two towns. If you choose to water and cultivate this plan, it will prosper. Mr. Big will move to a new destination if you so choose. He is very religious. His Muslim religion has suffered from the acts of the misguided. He wishes to change the way America sees the Muslim culture and spread goodwill to his American friends. His faith and interest in American enterprises has led him here to cultivate Muslim friendship. Mr. Big will share his enormous wealth with your towns, knowing the costs will be recovered as friendships kindle."

"Soon you will get to meet more Muslim friends from his entourage. It will be a cultural exchange. The time we spend here will enlighten your hearts."

The mayors only see one mighty rich dude. A special meeting, in the Executive Room, is arranged. The main players will now meet to discuss a strategy if the mayors buy into Mr. Big's plan. The mayors can develop business friendship with the man. At this meeting, greater project detail is provided.

Mr. Big is a giant of a man next to the two mayors. He lays out a drawing that outlines a river boat launch and building site along the river. A small boat livery with a couple of docks is complemented with an indoor sports complex, featuring indoor racquetball, volleyball, and a soccer field with seating for 2,000. An eighteen-hole golf course is shown nearby. As this massive drawing unfolds in front of the mayors, they become frozen figures. The splendor, color, and highlighted text in the drawing freeze the eyes of the two petrified mayors. They lean forward and are ready to hug Mr. Big. The mayors in unison read the large bold title, Mayors Conway and Michell Sports Complex. The blocked-print signs indicate retail stores in a section reserved for business enterprises. The two mayors are bowled over when Mr. Big waves to his lieutenant to unfurl the two handcrafted flags; each one is a monster flag, outlined in a nautical cast: fairport harbpr and grand river. Another lieutenant is wheeling out a carved, polished marble plaque with the inscription, "Dedicated to people of all faiths, From Mr. Big, Muslim sheik, 7-4-200X."

"Before your eyes, gentlemen, is a dream that you can make into a reality," says the big man.

Mr. Big is the man of the hour. His explanation is fast and convincing enough. He has outlined his plan and wowed our two unsuspecting mayors. Before them was the master drawing which detailed the reclamation project along the river. The land that laid barren for so long would be transformed into useful property. Instead of an industrial abandoned zone the land would be revitalized. The parchment was eloquently displayed on a golden easel. Mr. Big didn't quite stop his delivery. He had an additional present to give the mayors. Mr. Big hands each mayor an envelope that contains a reward for using good judgment. "You will meet my associate builder next."

The mayors are captivated by the drawing. They don't quite know how to accept all this promise. Grant Michell asks, "Would a contract be next?" Grant Michell is in a hurry to get this deal done. Mr. Big's attorney steps forward. He explains. "A contract is not necessary for Mr. Big is putting up all the money for the initial phase of the operation. He will assume all risk. He will use his wealth to simply pay for land ownership. Anything upgraded will be a private matter. You will provide the governmental help to obtain permits and deeds."

Mr. Big excuses himself by saying, "I must attend to other matters for a short while. The next part of our introduction will be a presentation from my friend, Lord Barrie. He is a man of many talents." As Mr. Big departs with his associates he introduces Lord Barrie. "Next up, I bring you greetings from my cast of company associates." Mr. Big holds his hand up to Lord Barrie.

"My name is Lord Barrie. I operate Barrie the Lion Builders, Inc. Please learn from the plan I will outline." The British accented gentleman says.

This closed door meeting continues in the back room with only our two mayors, Lord Barrie, and his lieutenants. His comments are British with an American slang used for effect. Nonetheless he's well-spoken. He tells the mayors of the many lands he's worked in. "I've constructed United Nations buildings in Libya, Morocco, and the Sudan on the African continent. I've built an office building for the newspaper, Izvestia, in Russia. My oil services background has helped me throughout the Middle East. I have an oil service operation in Saudi Arabia. I will bring in the large equipment here, along with the people to do phase one. This will be the earth development stage. An entire camp of people will stay at the site in order to keep operations flowing. The flow of equipment and supplies will progress in an orderly fashion, as has been the case with all my projects," Lord Barrie explains.

Mr. Big enters again and gives a traditional greeting to Lord Barrie. They hug each other, as the final part of the presentation concludes.

"That is a generous offer, Mr. Big," says Mayor Conway. "As we discussed the matter, we have concluded it would be a crime to pass up a venture such as this. Please mobilize your team and go to work."

"Mayors my lovely escorts will help attend to any needs a mayor may require." Mr. Big says. "I would rather not have any outside people muddling in this operation. As my letter indicates, I must have security and secrecy. I have some enemies of the past that I have beaten. I must continue to be on my guard."

Mr. Big instructs, "Watch over my lieutenants, they are here for my protection."

A lieutenant moves in such a way that his machine pistol is in plain view. Mr. Big says, "Please note my lieutenants are armed and they are instructed to protect my privacy. I insist I have your cooperation." He adds, "I have been in some tough fights in different countries. Force is needed at times. My way is to move into an area, develop, and move to another site. I'm sending around pictures of battles I've been in. You will see Lebanon, Egypt, and Jordan. After these battles, doors of opportunity open." Mr. Big explains, "With what I have said today, I must continue to emphasize the need for a personal area of secrecy. My spiritual habits require that I take time to pray. My faith is undaunted, as yours, Mayor Conway."

Mr. Big tells the mayor, "My troop is setting up a zone near where I intend to develop. We are in the process of success, as you will see. Last evening I made arrangements to stay with one of your locals. We will leave just as fast, if we are not welcome. In closing, honorable mayors, you're about to become famous."

That was just the words our two mayors needed to hear. Both are power drunk. The two mayors showed a sign of acceptance by shaking hands with Mr. Big. The wide smile across their faces testified to how happy they were. Mayor Michell is near tears. He walks over to the chalkboard and writes,

MR. BIG AND HIS PLAN
FAIRPORT HARBOR AND GRAND RIVER
"PROSPERITY"

The evening before the meeting with the mayors, Mr. Big arrived in town with an entourage of fancy mobile homes. He set up a mini-base of operation along the river near where he will kick off his plan. His limo is well endowed. As he exits his posh car, he gleans with pride. He has found a most appropriate base of operation.

The small-time marina operator runs out to meet these new travelers. A lieutenant greets the marina operator and says they are travelers and investors. "Sir, we have traveled a great distance and find this marina suitable to lodge in tonight. We will pay compensation to you for a right to bivouac an operation here. My leader would like to bid on taking control of this little-used marina. You will join our operation and retain your same capacity."

The operator of the marina is a bit overwhelmed by the forward, directed assault on his place of employment. This rundown marina and park is like home to him. Even though he's not the owner, he is the only caretaker and has worked at the marina for years. His pride is being infringed upon.

"Why, that is out of the question," says the operator. "I have six boaters tied up who are going to stay the summer. They own dock space here. How could I get the local boaters to leave at the beginning of boating season?"

Mr. Big, not far away, simply waves to his lieutenant. The lieutenant quickly pulls out a neat bundle of cash. A fist full of what looks like $100 dollar bills is quickly stuffed into the operator's pocket. A handgun is exposed to the operator. "Tell your boss we will need a lease to be signed promptly." The operator says, "I'll check with my boss. I don't see a problem with you fine folks."

The operator's face is flushed as he holds his breast pocket now bulging with bills.

"My boss is sure to like you. I think he's been wanting to retire and sell this marina. I don't think there will be a problem." The operator stumbles on his words as he is flustered. "It, that is, money has a way of curing what ails a deal." The operator has overcome his anxiety.

"Go ahead and park where you want. I'll turn on the power at the electrical outlets. You may be here a good while," The operator tells his interesting and rich guests. He's almost begging them to stay as long as they need too.

The operator quickly departs with a mad dash to the office. He flips on the circuit breakers to the outlets outside. Then he grabs the phone. He rarely has to call the owner and has to search for his phone number.

"Boss, Mack here. They can park at the camp for the next few days." Mack is so energized he steps ahead of the conversation. Smitty, the owner, can certainly hear Mack's excited voice as Mack conveys the situation to the boss. "Who is here, Mack? What are you talking about? Get a hold of yourself," Smitty demands. "Smitty, the nomads are here at your marina. They have something you like—money. This group is very upstanding. Something you're not used too. That get-rich scheme you always talk about has arrived," says Mack. "What in the hell are you talking about? I'm coming down there." Smitty barks over the phone.

Smitty doesn't believe Mack until he arrives at the business and Mack waves a wad of one hundred dollar bills at him. Smitty sees an orderly progression taking place as the newly arrived guests settle into the marina. "Well, I believe we can work something out," says Smitty as he rubs his hands together.

CHAPTER 7

❀

The Mission

The winter season will stop the shipping in Lake Erie. I watch the ice flows as they sail down the river and out into the lake. Boating is shut down too. The water temperature stays around a range of thirty-five to forty-five degrees Fahrenheit.

It's no wonder that one day a foreign group would locate to this soft underbelly. It is amazing that America is so free a land. People around the world are trying to gain access to our country. In the south, many illegal aliens are running roughshod over the border. The checks and balances of who is the good guy and who is the potential law breaker are seriously lacking. If Congress hasn't been watching what's going on down south, what's happening at other entry points? This massive border invasion has been going on through each administration. Democrats and Republicans both miss repairing an immigration policy gone mad. This need for inexpensive labor masks a growing problem. Can the average taxpayer afford the rich man's labor force and the problems it brings? Here in Ohio, we need a cheap labor force to help work the nursery industry. Lake County, Ohio, is home to the nation's nursery industry. Could it be home to a smoldering fire called terror?

Our neighbors to the north offer an entry point and an exit back to the nest. Canada can offer a springboard with which to carry out the work of Al-Qaeda. This foe has backing and the religion of fanaticism in their soul. Al-Qaeda is looking for the weak link in a crossing point through which the tools for annihilation can be shipped.

Fairport Harbor Port Authority Boat Ramp
Three Months Later

From a distance, I watch the boaters through the zoom lens on my camera. I see the port authority attendants keeping tabs on the boat traffic around the ramp.

The small boat ramp was buzzing with jet-ski riders, sailboats, and fishermen waiting to launch their watercraft. The Fairport Harbor Port Authority boat ramp was in business again after waiting out the cool springtime winds. Cool weather and windy conditions had put a damper on boating. Finally, the weather has broken. A warm weekend in early June is welcomed by all the patrons. People are just getting into the realization that summer is almost upon us. Fishermen are to the west of the sunbathers that are on the beach. They are next to each other but separated by the boat ramp's courtesy docks and a steel pier. This division of the beach people and the boaters keeps both groups from interfering with each other. The serious fishermen compete with the jet-ski boaters. In their minds, the fishermen have an unwritten priority to launch first. Their boats are usually much larger than a Jet Ski. From this perspective, it can take longer to launch a boat but that sometimes doesn't happen. The port authority doesn't assign any one group ahead of the other. The port authority has a separate jet-ski launch ramp. It can get backed up. The Jet-Skiers start moving over to the boat launch area and soon there's conflict. The ramp manager has to take control before tempers flair.

The hours in the day usually take care of who has a priority. The fishermen are early risers. The good ones shove off before 6:00 AM. After 8:00 AM the Jet-Ski crowd starts to show. By that time, most fishermen are well into their sport.

Salvador Cambello, the port authority operations manager and treasurer, stops at the ramp just before noon to check on the operations. He does much of the staff hiring. Ultimately, he will give the thumbs up or down on new hires. Each year the port authority picks attractive girls from the local high school to help with the sale of boat launch passes. Some boys are hired, but generally speaking, the port authority does better with girls. They are more responsible and the boaters react positively when asked to pay a launch fee. The girls can cause problems by having boyfriends congregating at the office and the usual distractions those close contacts can bring.

Customers can buy season passes or individual day passes from the attendants. The girls seem to provide a boost to sales each year. They also bring other problems unique to young people. Boyfriends and cell phones are just two of Sal's problems. Sal says he needs to keep a close watch on the girls because they can get distracted. He makes a point of checking in at least twice a day. He keeps close inventory of receipts and is quick to caution any off balance in the cash drawer. Handling public money is tricky business. Most of it is in small bills and pocket change. That can tempt anyone that doesn't have good ethics. All in all, the operation flourishes because of the closeness between the workers and management. This weekend day the work routine is becoming more intense. Today the girls have attracted the attention of the young Jet-Ski men. Of course, the fishermen like the girls too. Fishermen are always asking about the "hot spots." I'm sure they are talking about catching walleye and perch.

Sal, driving up to the main entrance, stays in his car as the ramp attendants come over to see him.

Sara mentions, "We have been getting rave reviews from the Jet-Ski boys." Cortney chips in, "Mr. Cambello, you need to give us a raise for our double duty. We're keeping the Jet Ski business booming *and* doing a good job at marketing your fishing stuff." Sal doesn't take long to come back with a one-liner. "You girls bring me two things, money and headaches. What's been going on today?" Sal asks. Jon says, "Welcome news, Mr. Cambello. A single yacht has paid to dock at the courtesy dockage this morning."

This is good news as the port authority needs to collect a return on their investment in docks.

Sal looks to see if the boat is still there. Sure enough, the yacht is still there. Cortney comments, "Mr. Cambello, the men on the yacht didn't say much, but they look kind of foreign, not like fishermen." Sal gives a look in the direction of the courtesy dock. His natural tendency, because he was a railroad inspector, is to check out the people using the facility.

He says good-bye to the girls as he drives past the boat unloading area and then swings around by the Jet Ski launch. There's only six or seven Jet-Ski customers using the launch area right now and about that many in the water. That will change as the afternoon will bring many more. Next, he heads to the courtesy dock for a look at the visitors. The boat that's there is pretty new. Sal doesn't want to disturb the boater. The girls are right. These guys are definitely dark skinned. Sal does a quick analysis. "They paid the fee to use the courtesy dock, that's good enough for me." With that thought, he turns his car around.

As treasurer and operations officer he's always protective of his paid patrons.

Sal heads back to the main entrance to the boat ramp. He has some parting words for the girls. "Girls, we all have to appreciate our patrons who use our boat ramp. I suspect we will have many visitors of different nationalities throughout the summer. As long as they don't cause problems, just take their money."

Sal waves at the girls as he departs down the asphalt road leading out of the facility. The road leading out of the port authority boat ramp is called Water Street. It was a bustling street back in the thirties because of the freighters coming into the harbor. Water Street businesses have dried up and moved out.

Sal is so glad the weather has turned favorable. All the work they have done at the ramp is starting to pay off now. He has put together another staff that will bring in the profits. This boat ramp is a cash cow. Sal whispers to himself, "If we only could keep the sand out of the ramp area. Dredging is a problem everywhere when the lake water level is low. The marina owners are crying to the port authority that their part of the river has a low water level. We all have this problem. Why can't the marinas just pay someone to dredge their area out? They have the big boats and make the big bucks. We have enough to do just running a boat ramp." He's bummed out by the thought of dredging the river. "I have enough to do."

As he turns up the hill leading off Water Street, he notices an old woman driving down. It's the port authority's competitor, Mrs. Mary Ann Rutherford. She owns a boat launch business upriver. She keeps her prices lower than the port authority. Sal says to himself. "She's checking up on her competitor, the Fairport Harbor Port Authority boat launch. She knows how to evaluate the enemy."

Mary Ann Rutherford will sit with her brother, John, for hours admiring the river's beauty. This grand lady has tested time. She's an entrepreneur extraordinaire. She recalls details that the average man may not see. She has river ears. She can hear sounds across the river as if the water telegraphs messages to her ears. She has an eye for detail, probably from her school-teaching past. That career has rewarded her in many ways. Her husband, himself a schoolteacher and administrator, has passed away long ago.

Mary Ann Rutherford drives up to the attendants. The girls realize she is just visiting and wave her through to turn around in the parking lot. Mary Ann drives along and stops to observe the action at the ramps. As she peruses the scenery she notices the yacht tied at the courtesy dock. She picks up her binoculars to get a better view. Thinking to herself, "These boaters aren't from around here." She knows most every yacht around. "That boat isn't familiar.

Those boaters don't know how to tie off a boat, either." She can see the mishmash knot they used to tie up the boat at the dock. "They are not sailors, either." Mary Ann is ready to head back to her boat ramp operation in Grand River. She puts her binoculars away and heads back home.

I saw enough to understand that our port authority boat ramp is in business again. I stash my camera in the case and walk home. The twenty-minute walk is refreshing as the temperature is turning out to be very warm.

Little does Richard know that the yacht parked at the courtesy dock is loaded with special equipment? A checklist of items on board includes an array of weaponry. Small caliber silent pistols, AK-47 automatic machine guns, and up to 75-millimeter mortars are hidden on board. These items are well concealed. These cell members will kill if the mission is threatened. A quantity of plastic explosives is stored in refrigerated coffee cans. The fire extinguishers are actually oxygen and hydrogen tanks. All of these tanks are repainted to give a false look of safety equipment. The scuba equipment onboard is well cared for and stowed away for future use.

There are more of these terrorist monsters around. Other cells are planted inland. Operating in the convenience store business, their mission is to stockpile various supplies as they are brought over from Canada. Money is laundered under the disguise of merchandising through these stores. The three stores in the area are well planted and have operated for some time now. The store cells have a fairly good handle on this section of the country. They wait quietly for messages from other supercell leaders. The stores' profits serve to pay for new arrivals. The real barbaric renegades will be arriving soon. They will need help to make their stay eventful.

The three men on the yacht open up their religious book and read passages. They have a little time to kill before planning starts in earnest. The yacht that is tied off at the courtesy dock has been parked for about three hours now. The courtesy dock has twenty places to tie up, although none are used but theirs. These guys use a remote dock area so as not to be disturbed by other boaters. They watch together as another boat pulls up alongside their yacht. It's a thirty-sixer.[1] A supercell leader instructs his crew to tie up to the smaller yacht. The three men on the yacht come aboard the thirty-sixer. Everybody is very businesslike. The men embrace in the customary manner of their culture. They immediately go into the cabin to discuss a battle plan. Only one guard is posted outside. He has a pistol ready for use. It is hidden from view.

---

1. Thirty-sixer refers to the length of the boat and the boats name

Cortney got a look at the newcomer yacht parked at the courtesy dock. "Someone needs to collect a user fee from that larger yacht," she said. The girls turn in unison and point to Casey. "It'll be Casey's turn to check on the new boat," the chorus of attendants exclaim. "Good grief, you guys." Casey replies. "I just came down to relieve one of you girls." "We elected you, Casey, to check on the newest arrival at the courtesy dock. It's your turn since you're just coming on duty," said Jon. Jenny and Sara share a comment to Casey, saying, "Don't get kidnapped." Casey just rolls her eyes.

Casey runs past the Jet-Ski guys. They let out a couple of catcalls, obviously in favor of her nicely tanned and shaped figure. She makes her way over to the yacht.

She yells over to the man standing guard on the boat. "Mister, I need to collect a user fee from you!" The guard listens and grumbles something to the men inside the cabin. Casey tries to make out what he is saying. She can't. She chalks up the difficulty in understanding his speech to the Jet-Ski motor noise in the area. A clean-cut man emerges and asks, "What do you need, young lady?" "How long are you staying?" Casey asks. He says, "Four to eight hours." She shows him a two and five fingers. "Twenty-five bucks," She says.

She can understand him just fine. He reaches into his wallet and peels off a fifty. "Keep the change," he replies. "You can stay as long as you need to sir," Casey says. "Thank you, young lady," the man replies.

Casey bolts off with the money. She's got to tell the others of her big tipper.

"Thanks for giving me that customer. He just gave me a twenty-five dollar tip," Casey says. "It's time to celebrate. It's pizza time. I'm buying, girls, you're included Jon." Casey puts the money in the cash register and pockets the tip. She grabs the pizza menu they have used and calls in the order.

The three men who came on board the thirty-sixer for the meeting have maps of the area. They detail some ideas they have with the supercell leader. They came from the other side of the lake and have a good collection of landmarks to use for navigational purposes. A timeline was created that will be used to plan an attack and escape back to Canada. It was a sixty-two-mile trip for them from Canada. The thirty-foot boat made the trip with ease. This test voyage was conducted to set conditions for a more momentous trip in the future. Future trips will bring in supplies and reinforcements to bolster the operation. The men in the small yacht have surveyed the shoreline. They would use the survey to carry out a future exploratory mission at the nuclear power plant.

Ahmed al Sahed, the bomber and navigator, explains, "The power plant to the west and the Perry nuke plant stick out along the shoreline. Towers and smoke stacks are clearly seen from a distance. We have a can't-miss visual identification. The water system here in Fairport Harbor is an easy target but of low value. My expertise should be used at the high value target." Ahmed casts his eyes in the direction of the nuclear power plant.

The Perry Nuclear Power Plant casts a pillow of steam high into the air. It's about ten miles east of this boat ramp. The white plume of steam provides a guiding landmark.

The bomber thinks that the power plant will be the target. Abu el Kuri, the group leader of the thirty-foot yacht, says, "Our leaders may decide we need to have that nuclear plant on our target list. We don't know the security around the plant but we can travel by boat near there and pretend to fish. We know few of the fishing habits of the residents here but that will be our cover to test if they are watching for intruders. Another in the group adds a logistical point. "First, we will need to refuel our boat before we test the security at that power plant," says Saheed Ahmed, the youngest member on the boat.

"A supercell leader is planning to meet with other associates at a restaurant down the river," says the main terrorist, Captain Awad. He is the senior leader of this pack. He has many roles to fill. Coordinator, planner, leader are his main duties. Captain Awad, tells them, "You three take your boat down river and look over the salt company mine on your way to refuel. This may be another target. I have made arrangements for you to off load your equipment to a white van up river. You will be signaled by your brothers. Go after our prayers." They pray together and the meeting wraps up.

The men get back on their boat. They now intend to drive by future targets several times. Right now they have a more pressing appointment to make, off load the hardware and notably, get some fuel. They will take notes of the harbor as they head upstream.

A trip up the Grand River was already planned by Captain Awad. His boss, Mr. Big, will have his operation in full swing well up the river. Mr. Big's construction tent is next to the river. He has a crew working on landscape and other members working on the final answer. This big tent covers another tent that houses a tunnel. This mine and shaft goes down about 200 feet so far. The work is beginning to slow because of a water problem. The excavation crew encountered a heavy water leak from an underground spring.

All parts of a growing system of cells are beginning to meet each other. Captain Awad must get to William Tell's restaurant around 2:00 PM. This will be between the rush of lunchtime diners and the supper crowd. Off goes the thirty-sixer.

I watched a convenience store worker change her makeup and style of dress over the last year. The reason I bring this up is I'm starting to get suspicious of certain people. I stop at this out-of-the-way store to buy beer every so often. At first I thought this person was just trying to come of age with the American dress code. When I first saw her, she was wearing the clothing of a Middle-Eastern woman. She was like someone from Saudi Arabia. Now she has makeup on, rather overdone. She seems to run the show at the store. The new people I see there can't speak English. I start to question my gut feeling. "I'm just paranoid," I say.

I go to the river and the lake to take pictures pretty often. I'm an amateur digital photographer. During my photo sessions I have a chance to see what is going on around the lake. My sightings of odd fellows, a man wearing a turban on the beach, and other men milling around certain stores start to scribe an indelible print in my investigative mind. My paranoia is getting the best of me. "I got a phobia," I say. "Heck, everyone's coming to America. We have an open house." I know I'm being facetious, but deep down I'm a little edgy.

Grand River

CHAPTER 8

❀

Gotta Keep a Secret

I caught a huge break when I spied the letter to the mayor on Horst Beamer's desk. For once I'm in the know. I can't reveal any of this information to port authority board members or the public. I just don't feel right about the way I scooped the info. "The mayor and his staff must have this problem too. They keep many things secret, especially tax secrets," I say to myself, half joking.

Unknown to the other port authority board members, the mayors are sworn to secrecy regarding Mr. Big's plan. Our mayors certainly don't want to lose this big-time spender. A developer of Mr. Big's stature hardly comes but once in a lifetime.

Richard, in his nightmares, has seen some disturbing graphics about to be bestowed upon the two unsuspecting communities. His daydreams have alarmed him, especially the one about Mr. Columbo. He puts the dreams and nightmares together in a mental file. He hasn't been able to comprehend whether these dreams are true visions. He could be hallucinating from the effects of long-term alcohol abuse. He is not sure.

The two mayors are winning accolades from the public for their work in restoring a shine to the village's image. It is not necessary to tell the mayors that they are doing a magnificent job. They have been in the newspaper headlines. New residential development is taking place under their command. They have new development in the long-range plans. The village councils are satisfied with the progress seen so far. The sweet smell of success is overwhelming.

"Freedom to think, write, and act without intrusion is under assault. Writing about one's belief and being open is right. We should not have a government conniving in back room deals. We have a government ready to sneak one in on the unsuspecting citizens."

I'm talking to myself while standing in front of the bathroom mirror. "I must take the time to discuss this issue at length. This is where our small towns must be careful." I take a gulp of Molson's Canadian as if it's mouthwash. "Here I am trying to explain to myself. The town mayor in Grand River should never be sitting on the same port authority board to which he appoints members. Grant Michell is making a big mistake. The possibility of misuse of power will exist if this is permitted. This is especially true if the mayor is contributing to writing tax law for the port authority and sitting on the port authority board. Worse still, the mayor is president of a port authority board and he appoints the board members. How could this ever happen under Ohio law? Where is county scrutiny?"

"It's time for a cold one," I say.

The effect is the same. I continue my drinking session and reach a point where it's time to lay down. "How can I explain this odyssey?"

I'm nearly passed out and reach a point where I start to dream again.

What's going on here? I see Rick and the Erie Indian. Rick is close to the Indian but slightly hidden. The two are maybe fifteen yards apart. The Indian has an aim directed at the lion. The Indian follows the lion's movement with the bow and arrow.

Rick is in the cover of the cattail stalks near the river. The lion is jumping from a large passenger boat, on which he's just ravaged the people on board.

Rick moves the cattails and the Indian looks over to him. This distraction causes the lion to bolt. The startled lion is on land, running full speed parallel to Rick and the Erie Indian.

Suddenly, as I wake up, I'm pushing away the covers on my bed as if I'm coming out of the dense cover of the river. "Jesus, Rick made him miss or was it me?" The dream is fresh in my mind. "I should write this down," I say.

My legs are cramping as if I was squatting down for the last hour. I crawl over to the bathroom and lift myself up to my knees. I reach for a bottle of aspirin as I work to stand. My buttocks muscles hurt where my legs meet my butt. I turn on the water and use my hand to scoop up a palm full of water to wash down two aspirin.

"I know that dream means something. I have to find out what." I walk back to my bed. I can smell the presence of the river from my open window. I lay back down to rest my aching legs. I'm too tired to write down what just happened.

"This is really weird," I say as I go back to sleep.

I wake up the next morning and start thinking about the past.

The Erie Indians inhabited this area and they left artifacts around. My uncle Steve took me to a site to dig for Native American souvenirs. I was only eight or nine years old at that time. It was around 1959 when I was digging with my uncle. I learned later on that the Erie Indians were residents in this area.

An archeological team came to Fairport Harbor to examine an old Indian burial ground. This was located next to the rebuilt North St. Clair Street Bridge. Blowing up the old bridge was a shock to the river. Those old burial grounds hold secrets of this Grand River and its legacy. These sacred Native American burial grounds were violated. This was where my dream took place last night.

I can't say how all this ties together. At least not right now. I have another fact about this area. I recall along our river we chose to add a little bit of this and a little bit of that. Before the EPA came along, a Fairport Harbor dumping zone was created. It was enormous in size where residents could dispose of their garbage. It covered a quarter mile. It was also next to the Grand River, right by the Indian burial grounds.

My body was still sore from the way I slept last night. I told myself I must have been chasing Indians through the night.

I finished a couple of photo jobs and decided to reflect on my dream at the neighborhood bowling alley. It's late Saturday afternoon. I'm sitting in the local bowling alley thinking about the latest sports line instead of my dreams. I have to place a wager on tomorrow's baseball games with Salvador Cambello's friend. The local barmaid, Busty, and the bar owner, Bruno, provided a few jokes and we cut the card to see who will be the lucky person to buy the next round. After a few social brews, a vision slowly creeps into my mind. *I see that lion again.* I don't understand the symbolism. I need to break away from the bowling alley bar. I'm slightly frightened, fearing that this time the dream will become more intense. I keep my head down so no one can see my face. I don't want the bar patrons and Busty thinking I'm losing my cool. I walk to the restroom to calm down. The restroom has a mirror above the sink. As I look in the mirror, the Erie Indian stares back at me. That was enough beer for me. I walked back to the bar. "I better go, Busty, the beers are clouding my mind. I have way to much port authority on my mind."

Busty, at twenty-five years old, would normally have kept me drinking for another couple beers. This time I wasn't sticking around. I'm seeing Indians in the mirror and I still had a meeting to attend that evening.

The Great Sail Marina meeting was my first real test dealing with the public. The boaters were complaining about the water level. I listened to their problems as a good official should. I told them I would report what they had to say to the other board members. I invited them to our meeting. I could see the dredging problem was gaining momentum.

**The Grand River splits the two villages of Fairport Harbor and Grand River
The river was shallow throughout this area**

CHAPTER 9

❀

Picking Up a Sign

Mary Ann is watching the river traffic go by and is mesmerized by the choppy water. As if she is in another time zone, she recalls a dream. She wonders, "I was sitting alone in William Tell's restaurant." She's confused. "Why was I sitting at a back table?" She has a particular spot where she sits and the hostess will always guide her to that area. For some reason, in her dream she was sitting in a completely different spot. As she snaps out of the daydream, she asks herself, "Why is this river playing tricks on me? The Grand River is playing a game with me. Why did this river just coach me into such a compelling thought?" She doses off again and starts to dream.

She decided to have a late lunch at William Tell's and see if visiting the restaurant will jog her memory about a past business adventure. "The coffee they serve there will open my mind. The river is such a powerful force of nature," she remarks.

"John," she says, "the river is telling me to pay a visit to William Tell's." She once owned that premier restaurant. That was one of her darling financial dealings way back when.

Brother John remarks, "You don't need an excuse to rub elbows at William Tell's."

Her business at the boat ramp was pretty good today. Her brother is keeping tabs on the boat launch so she can take a late lunch. She walks over to William Tell's restaurant. She decided to sit alone in the back because a restaurant worker was running the vacuum in her regular dining section. The place she picks out is out of the spotlight. The lighting is dim where she is sitting, but she has a good fix on everyone else that comes to dine. The lighting is not so low that she can't read the afternoon newspaper. Lunchtime customers are filing out. There is a shifting of clientele. The straggler customers come in now. These are the boaters who overslept or were too hung over to get up in the morning.

The coffee is tasting mighty good today. She seems to be inspired as the caffeine rush is giving her a second wind. Her eyes are fine-tuned on the small procession of late diners.

Some customers file in and sit down a few tables away. The group of five is seated away from everyone else accept Mary Ann. "They must want to be by themselves too. The one fella must be a basketball player. He's a big man." She's thinking.

Mary Ann is one person that has an eye for detail, today as every day. She muses over the way the three ladies with the men have cropped their hair. Mary Ann has experience in the hair-styling business from long ago. She started a school for cosmetologists back in the early fifties. She's thinking these three girls are unusual for other reasons. They don't seem to know each other. The wardrobe is flashy and their makeup is overdone. It's not that foreign-looking people don't come to Ohio. Grand River restaurants attract a fair amount of patrons from other places.

As they talk, their language is broken. Mary Ann can't get a fix on the whole of the conversation because of the distance from her table. The whine of the vacuum isn't helping. Suffice to say these folks aren't Mexican. "They could be Eastern European, maybe Russian." She thinks. "These girls have a rigid posture, almost soldier-like in their demeanor. They aren't being social." The man sitting next to the big man keeps motioning to the girls to calm down. Mary Ann is careful to shield her eyes with the paper. She certainly doesn't want to be caught staring. The fact is she can almost read their lips. The whole group at the table seems to be a mixed bag of third-world characters. Two of the girls have matching tattoos. The exposed tattoo of a lion on their open-neck, silk shirt gives them the look of gang members, yet their earrings are all ruby red. Mary Ann strains her ears to record their voices. The accent is unmistakable. "Definitely, the women are Russian."

These folks are soon joined by two other men. Again it's more of the same. Foreign-looking men, possibly Middle Eastern or Mediterranean folks, I believe. Mary Ann is sure she saw one of them on a yacht not long ago. This group is part of the bad-knot boys. They don't know how to tie off a boat to a dock. The greeting they extend to one another is a foreign custom, she reckons. As she listens in, the sounds of broken dialect come through. The girls are babbling on. They stumble *on simple words off the menu. She can see the one guy is looking at her so she returns to her paper reading.*

"I better get back to the boat launch and help my brother, John," she tells the waitress. Mary Ann passes by the table of foreigners and recognizes a faint smell of incense. Another waitress is bringing over cups of tea. She nods to Mary Ann. Back at the boat launch she takes her seat by her brother. "John, William Tell's lunchtime customers are like a meeting at the United Nations." She relates the lunchtime news to her brother. She says, *"The foreigners are invading."*

Mary Ann wakes up from a nap and looks at her watch. It's an hour later.

"Wow, what a dream, John. That's my memory playing tricks on me." She tells her brother, "I remember those people. It was a month ago that those foreigners were in the restaurant." John shrugs his shoulders and shakes his head as if to say, "What are you talking about?" Mary Ann finishes by saying one last comment, "My sense of self-security tells me something is not quite right with those people." John says to Mary Ann, "You better take another nap. You got up on the wrong side of the boat dock."

Mary Ann and John resume their guardianship of the river. They watch the boaters who are returning from a day's adventure on the lake. Most of her customers are season-pass holders. They launch and retrieve their boats without any assistance. That's just fine with Mary Ann and her brother John. It is time for an afternoon siesta.

CHAPTER 10

Security and Safety

Last year I was doing routine inspections at the Fairport Harbor port authority boat ramp, when a group of four men in their twenties were having Jet-Ski problems. The attendant asked me to check on this group. She believed I could help our customers. I agreed, and shuffled over to see for myself how I could help. I didn't expect to need a translator. These boys weren't Mexican and for some reason I sensed danger at the time. Their foreign flavor suggested they were Middle Eastern or European. I tried to communicate with them and some measure of relief came to me when one of them talked with me. His English was fair. They had a bigger problem getting their Jet Ski fixed and whatever else they wanted to do was on the back burner. The fact that we were having a difficult time communicating was probably nothing to worry about. Deep down, I had a nervous feeling. I was definitely disturbed without outwardly showing my concern. They had an advantage. I remember when a couple of them did talk I didn't know what was being said.

I worked about two hours on freeing the prop and drive shaft of twisted polypropylene line. They must have run over a buoy marker and the line traveled up into the prop and drive shaft. I used my American ingenuity. After several lame attempts to cut the rope using a knife, I used my soldering gun and melted through a blob of tangled rope. I didn't stick around to see them leave.

My memory serves me well on this group. They seem to have more on their mind than just Jet Ski matters. The girls at the ramp were attracting their attention. That was another thing I remember.

Problems are always the case at the ramp. Problems with motors, boats, batteries are normal.

Right now thinking to myself, I realized how difficult it must be to travel on an airliner, a subway, or train. The language barrier was what made me feel uneasy. I'm the one with the problem.

I reflect on how the world is today. "This world we live in now is disturbing. We have to confound these terrorists or they will run around the world making trouble wherever they are free to roam. If we don't confront this threat, it will mutate in a more dangerous way. Life has plenty of ordinary problems. Giving murderers, thieves, and terrorists a free place to hide and plan is unconscionable. We need to use all the tools in the box. What do we have to lose? It is all about our way of life. Freedom has always come at a price. Soldiers die on the battlefield, so that the next generation lives in a free society. I understand that a military must always sharpen the sword and have it ready to checkmate the next menace. It wasn't that long ago that Hitler rose to power. Now another group has sprung up. It is the Bin Laden group. Take a look around the world and see the result of their rise to power. Countries all over the world are suffering from bombings, surprise attacks, and suicide murders. The enemy of mankind walks into a public place with a death belt of dynamite to terrorize. Terrorists have killed their own people to rationalize some twisted meaning of life and religion. They dictate to the world how we have to believe. Free nations must stand tall, together, to stop this invasion of freedom." I finally break my stream of consciousness by recalling some past problems at the boat ramp.

The port authority has had many different folks use the ramp. One time a fist fight erupted between a little guy and the stocky, tall guy. The heavyweight tough talker could have told the little guy he should take his best shot. Murder on his hands would not be in his best interest. It really looked like a serious mismatch. After arguing about who should ramp first, the argument flamed up. A pushing and shoving match brewed. Next, along come the fists making direct hits. The little guy overwhelms the heavyweight with concentrated blows to the face and head and the tall guy is down. The tall guy yields to the golden glove guy.

On another occasion, a boater is backing his boat up to launch. He forgets to set the parking brake or the parking brake just didn't hold and in goes the Chevy Blazer. That SUV just isn't built to float. This takes out one of the launch ramps at the most busy time of the day. There are hundreds of stories to tell at the boat ramp. The previous ramp manager did a good job containing problems. The godfather's next ramp manager finds the boat ramp a nice challenge. Husband and wife team work very hard at keeping the boat ramp safe. The ramp manager sees a lot. The interesting fact is that we never know too much about our patrons. I'm sure we could use a surveillance system at the boat ramp. We just don't have the money for that type of security.

Well along comes September 11, 2001. I bet Logan Airport wishes they had the money for better security. I think to myself now how vulnerable we are on the southern shore of Lake Erie. Anyone entering this harbor will probably go unnoticed. Based on what I know about our boat ramp, anyone can get in. This is why I want the county sheriff looking over the security of the harbor.

We have a salt mine on the other side of the river and water systems right next to the boat ramp. The nuclear power plant not to far away. All potential targets for mischief. Good for us that we have the coast guard station close by. The U.S. Coast Guard is a welcome member to the security team on Lake Erie. Shallow Lake Erie will kick up when the winds blow and overwhelm the unsuspecting boater. I would prefer that Sheriff Clayton Miller have his people study conditions around the harbor. Maybe they have a plan to intercede if called upon to neutralize a real menace. I know that my brief encounter with people who don't speak English made me feel uneasy. Will I see the U.S. Navy standing by at this harbor someday? God only knows.

Oh well, life goes on here. Who needs to pay attention to who visits our area? Now, that may be more necessary than ever. Seems that in the Middle East, the suicide bomber is more interested in dining establishments, and we have some nice ones in Grand River. Are the freighters that stop at the harbor scrutinized? Is terror at our doorstep?

It couldn't happen here. Probably not and we don't need to spend a lot of time on it. I only mention it for the fact that I ran into characters that were different.

Someone planning bad things may spend some time investigating this area. We get so many different people visiting. It would be hard to pick out the evil plotter. I would like to have trained people in place to deal with any threat. High school students work at the boat ramp as attendants. Sara, Jenny, Cortney, Michelle, Jon, Sharon, and Casey were good for the boat ramp. Could they pick out a terrorist? Now other high school kids are down there. We all want a little better heads up on who is pulling into our ramp. Who could provide better coverage and public service? That is the question.

Here again is a point about security that we seem to miss. This day and age it is important to be ready to recognize the danger signs of the times. Fairport Harbor's 'Mayberry' police department may not be up to the task working with only two roving patrol cars. No one will fault them, as they are a good bunch of part-time officers. They do a good job throughout the town. The police force is busy with traffic tickets and investigating minor criminal activity. Most of these police officers move on to greater challenges. Their sights are on better paying positions.

Police Chief Otto Mueller has enough work to do in town. His people respond to the boat ramp problems that occur over the season of boating. Could he and his men be expected to challenge a group of terrorists? I know the answer.

CHAPTER 11

Tax and Politicians

"Move over, port authority, the mayors are going to come up with a plan to fix the Grand River. What we have here is a plan of opportunity. We are going to help the boaters that use Grand River," said Mayor Reese Conway.

So begins the trek of two village mayors seeking to find a common way to tax the boaters in their respected jurisdictions. Will they achieve fairness by taxing boaters who lease dock space at the marinas? Could they levy a user fee on boaters because they drive up and down the river? These ideas are tossed about over and over. The "Richard doctrine" is that if fairness to all boaters is a goal, then the political apparatus should have the county work up a system that we can all live with. The county can then send to the port authority a measure of tax to support harbor reclamation and maintenance.

Richard is making noise again about this Grand River user fee. Richard's theme, as was Mr. Columbo's speech at the marina, was to establish a county port authority. A tax administered by the county is best administered by the government capable of handling such a tax. Fairport Harbor and Grand River Village didn't have the wherewithal to accomplish collecting a tax. The mayors wanted to distribute the revenue to each port authority. Hammering on the fact that the two towns don't have facilities or a system to collect a tax or user fee, Richard has become the loose cannon of the mayoral appointments.

He preaches to the marinas to support a user tax. When that idea lost momentum or was frowned upon, he went in another direction. "My plan is a single, one-time collection," he says at the Great Sail Marina. "This would be manageable." The marina is filled with boaters from all associations. They seemed to accept this one time collection. Richard was ecstatic. Most everyone would go along with this plan.

I was gaining support with my idea and also the fear of public speaking was subsiding in me. I knew my political future was hanging by a thread. Each time I talked with the mayor, I felt as if I was on a tree limb watching him saw away at the branch.

The user fee idea, for Grand River maintenance and dredging, was proposed long ago. Back in the eighties, when Richard was first on the port authority board, he discussed this with another bunch of board members. These clever men had the right idea, but they lacked the political clout to implement this tax plan. These intelligent guys were all veteran port authority board members, and I was the newcomer. Each time this user fee idea came up the board just couldn't figure out how to collect it. We would call in the lawyer to rule on the legality. He would say, "Both towns share the river. Both port authorities from each town have to agree to tax the boaters equally. You can't collect a user fee on one side without collecting a fee on the other side." He was probably right, but I always thought he had a boat moored in one of the marinas and certainly didn't want to pay a user fee. Because the river was shared equally with the Grand River village, a plan to tax the boaters was tabled every time it came up at port authority board meetings.

Now these two mayors must realize that taxing issues are going to spark a war. Richard is still convinced that letting the boaters volunteer their own contributions to dredging is still the best way. If you can't afford to pledge money for your own dredging, then sit on the shore with your boat. If you can't leave the dock because the water level is too low, then you need to deepen the river. Hello. When do you need to tax yourself to decide if you need to dredge? Take a look at your boat. If it's hitting the bottom of the river, it's time to dredge. If your section of the river needs to be dredged, then you should be saving up to do it. This was a common theme that he spoke at marina meetings.

Fortunately, Richard has made plenty of contacts with the average boaters. He has convinced the majority of boaters to dredge the river by using an existing state grant and a pool of private money collected by the marinas. Mary Ann Rutherford provided the seed money. She put up $50,000. Sensing a lack of support, the mayors backed down on their tax scheme. The Grand River boaters voted the tax down and Fairport Harbor village boaters voiced their opinion and down went the user fee. Richard was satisfied with collecting a one-time voluntary fee. This fee was paid to the treasurer, Salvador Cambello.

CHAPTER 12

Communication

Communication was very important to the boaters. Many times Richard would visit with individuals and groups. Keeping a constant platform to speak from was the best plan. Richard made some good inroads with the boaters. Back at the port authority board meetings, Richard delivered enough information about dredging and the feelings of the boaters. Richard told the board he was keeping a line of communication open between the boaters and the board.

As the dredging project became increasingly grooved and on track the right people started to come on board. The wrong people suddenly and miraculously changed color. Board members Sal Cambello and Victor Tomlinson changed their tune. They did not want the port authority to be involved with dredging the river. They said it would bankrupt the port authority. I call them the right boat people now because they provided some push when they recognized the fact that this project could be done. Sal Cambello said the marinas are sending him money to deposit in an account for dredging. He liked the fact that the boaters trusted him with their money. This may have been the ticket that changed his tune. Naturally, Victor switched his view.

I wanted to talk about harbor security but I couldn't work that into the conversation when talking about dredging. Dredging was a key issue but really a secondary concern of mine. I was convinced that this dredging project was a way to reach the boaters and other governmental bodies. If I could get the county to look into the port authority dredging business, I might be able to raise the harbor security issue with them.

When I called the mayor and told him the marinas will volunteer their own money to help with the dredging project, he figured he could salvage some political points. After losing the user fee vote, he may as well join in and take some credit for securing dredging funds. In this particular case, the mayors came along for the ride because they were out of touch with the boaters. Realizing the boaters are voters and the dredging project was maturing, the mayors' incentive to be involved increased. They needed to get a handle on how it was progressing. Certainly, a politician is going to want to be recognized. This project was getting attention. That meant it was getting headlines. The local newspaper, the *Lake County Voice*, was very valuable. Because river dredging generated public interest, we all know who was going to be ready to take their bows.

The mayor arranged to be at key meetings. I must admit he knows the right people because the local newspaper and politicians in Columbus were coming to help with the dredging project. It went from nowhere at first to full speed ahead when the *Lake County Voice* started to talk it up. The newspaper reporters were on top of this local story.

Richard kept up a constant communication with engineers and managers of the Army Corps of Engineers and the Ohio Department of Natural Resources. Ohio was committing the largest share of the grant.

At the village hall people started to talk about Richard. The mayor and his assistants didn't want that guy grabbing the headlines. He's really going to get it done. "That guy is getting all the headlines. We're not in the limelight," a citizen hears Mr. Beamer say. A politician is more worried about his or her headlines than they are about getting a job done. When you want someone to run your business, find a doer, not a politician.

Being an appointed board member and a doer makes Richard a poor candidate for political office. He answers to the mayor. If he voices an opinion that is counter to the mayor's wishes, he could find himself out of this appointed office. Right there, what you see is the danger. A board member on the port authority almost has to be a yes man. He or she is a one-term doer or lives a lifetime in the box.

Inside the Executive Chamber was where Richard and other past board members heard a provocative statement. A mayor told them, "You do things my way or resign." That was explained to him under another regime. Richard thinks he's going to be put in irons and sealed away. Richard always said, "It isn't easy being me."

Richard needs to have some balance in his life so that if he's put out of Fairport Harbor politics, he can move on. He starts to expand his photography business. He starts to connect to God by praying. His spiritual contact with God becomes meaningful. By being closer to God, he can achieve balance in his life. Richard does not stop his alcohol use. He prays for another chance to get the message out about terrorism. The chance comes quickly.

CHAPTER 13

❀

Another Chance

Call it fate or chance that I was working in the yard as Mayor Conway came walking by. We exchanged greetings. I was uncomfortable knowing that he and I were not on the same page in our view of port authority structure. I wanted one more opportunity to tell him the county port authority idea is needed for security reasons. I just didn't think we were keeping up with the times.

This unofficial meeting presented me with an opportunity to share with him my hospitality. "Mayor Conway, how about a cool beverage. You're probably on mile number two." He hesitated, and accepted my invitation. "OK, I'd like to take a break," he said.

"Beer OK, mayor?" I asked. "Why not? But just one," he answered. Boy, have I heard that one. I figured the beer would loosen up our minds. I didn't tell him this beer would be my fourth.

"I have a little planting to do, mayor. A few tomato plants need to get in the ground. I'll never catch up with yard work. There is no way I could be a farmer. Every year I try something new, all I get is weeds. The one year when I had what I considered a nice garden growing among my weeds, my son came over and volunteered to cut the lawn. He was thorough. He ran the lawnmower over my garden. He butchered what plants I had growing, but that year I grew great weeds. Actually, he did a nice job on the lawn," I related.

We got a good laugh at that one. I was on a roll. Out of the blue, I was struck with a vision. It was a terrorist attack in my daydream. *Two women are going to blow up the mall.* I can't believe this. The vision came and went quickly. I shuddered.

The mayor asks, "Richard, are you OK?

I know my face was flushed. The pause in our discussion was a giveaway that I had wandered into an unknown space, a loss of consciousness. I needed to make a comeback statement. "I'm winded from the gardening." I said.

"Are you sure it's not the sauce." He was obviously referring to the beer. Maybe he knew I had a few already.

"Mayor, you're not going to believe this. Oh, never mind." I said. I lost my nerve to say what was really happening.

I quickly changed into a cover-up mode. "I've got a medical situation," I said "The medicine I'm taking sometimes reacts when I exert myself." I lied.

"Why don't you join me for lunch this afternoon, I'll buy," I said.

He thought about my request and agreed. He said he would drive. With that he finished his beer and told me he would pick me up in an hour.

This was my lucky break. I'm going to expel, come clean, and clear the air. I'll share all of my thoughts about the port authority. I'm going to bring up the regional port authority plan. I'll blend in the county port authority plan. This is something this area needs. "Is the beer doing the talking?" I ask myself. "He's going to see right through me." I mutter to myself, "Blasted, I'm all mellowed from the beer. Security is our number one problem this day and age. I'm going to hammer on that topic"

I realize he's probably not going to give in on my port authority vision. He's a college guy. He's suited for the mayoral office, whereas I'm a regular Joe. He knows better and he could be right. My problem is I'm getting a darn message from God.

"It's the beer, boob," I exclaim and sink into a depressed state.

I pop open another beer. Oh, I might as well build up my courage, I think. This meeting will be cool in the fact that I can say I rubbed elbows with the mayor. The port authority board will think I'm kissing the mayor's butt.

I was starting to get a little drunk. The mayor pulled up one hour to the minute of our previous talk. He was astutely dressed. I, of course, had changed into a casual regular Joe.

"Mayor, don't take me to one of those executive clubs." Let's keep things affordable. You're a high roller and I'm an alley cat."

"Don't worry; we'll have a good time. I know a spot in Mentor near the mall where the waitresses are classy and the food is decent," he reassured me.

I'm thinking to myself that I've heard stories about the mayor and his appetite for fine women. "Hey, this could mean I'm going to get lucky. I just know this is going to cost me a Franklin. A hundred bucks blown on an afternoon dinner, I'm insane. Richard, you ass," I say to myself.

I quickly regroup. My senses are dull, and I've got an afternoon buzz on from the beer.

The mayor is a great host. He can carry a conversation. He is a true politician.

We chitchat along the way, and unexpectedly I notice a white van. The two occupants are women in their twenties, maybe. Suddenly, it hits me again. I'm mesmerized by the whole picture. *A white van, women, and something else is beaming to me.*

"Mayor, I don't know where you're going but do me a favor. Please, follow that white van. It's important, trust me."

The mayor sees the woman at the wheel. He doesn't have a problem with this. He says, "You know, Richard, you're not a twentysomething guy anymore."

I can't tell him what's going on with me right now. I think those two women are going to the mall to cause a great calamity. The spell on me was powerful. I had to follow my instincts this time.

"Mayor, stay within sight of that van. You'll understand shortly." I exclaim.

"Mayor, this picture in my mind is telling me we should follow that white van. It has something to do with you. You're going to become a national news item." I figured telling him that will inflate his head. After all he's a politician, they live for the spotlight.

I've had all those beers. My body is starting to tell me I better think about looking for a men's room, but we have to stay close to these two ladies.

We travel across the railroad bridge and sure enough the van turns toward the mall. The driver of the van is careful not to speed. The van pulls into the mall and heads toward the food court entrance. It parks well away from the food court entrance. Both of the women step from the van. They're hot. I know this has got the mayor's attention. He hasn't said anything yet as he slows up. He's doing a case study of what I'm doing.

"Mayor, stop a few rows away. I'm going to ask them what they are up too. You probably want me to ask them to join us." Only kidding, I add, "I'll set us up with a double blind date." The mayor nods his head in approval.

I spring from the car and wave to the women.

This is getting serious. I'm truly afraid.

"Girls, I'm a reporter doing a story," I shout. "Could you stop for a second?"

They are a good forty yards away as they spin around to see who is talking to them. They spot me waving my arms. They don't waste any time hightailing back to the white van. Instantly, it starts, and they are off. I can see the passenger is out of her seat.

I scramble back to the mayor's car. "Follow them, mayor" I command. He's not sure what to do. "Reese, go." I demand. He hesitates as the white van is pulling away. It drives a short distance and stops by a Salvation Army dumpster and then takes off.

The mayor is still dumbfounded. He puts the car in gear and is not sure what to do. I'm rooting for him to go. "Move it, mayor, move it."

The mayor asks. "Are you nuts? What in the world are you trying to do? You scared those two away. Some blind date. I'm going to handle thing from here. You need to calm down. Try a couple of deep breathing exercises. Those girls didn't do anything. What was the problem?"

I felt ashamed as I sunk into the bucket seat. I was ready for a confrontation with the babes. They just blew out of the parking lot after stopping by the dumpster.

The mayor drove along for about three minutes and then a boom goes off. I'm wondering to myself, "What happened?" "Go back to the mall, mayor." I plead.

"No way, man, you're drunk," he said.

I'm ashamed to admit it. He's right.

The mayor isn't going back to the mall. He says they'll pick us up for harassment. "Whatever happened back there will just get us into the wrong kind of news. Richard, your lady tactics are in dire need of a transfusion."

We have lunch at a popular restaurant. It was uneventful. My opportunity failed me. I know I was on to something. I didn't get to raise the question about the port authority. The white van episode went sour. My credibility took another hit. My life is just melting.

CHAPTER 14

❀

Smoke and Fire

I made a guest appearance at the Fairport R & B & R Fishing Association. The place was packed with fishermen and women. All the seats were filled and the standing room area was shoulder to shoulder with people. The president of the association ran through his opening ceremonies and turned over the meeting to me.

These hard-core fish catchers and boaters were happy to hear from a port authority member. I was drumming up support from the area boaters. They were appreciative of the update about the dredging project.

"The Fairport Harbor Port Authority is working very diligently on finding new revenue streams to help fund the Grand River dredging project," I lied. The only one working on finding new revenue streams was me. "We need the support of all the boaters, fishermen, and sailors who use the Grand River. When I say support, I am talking about a voluntary contribution. I mean have each member contribute to a fund for dredging. The marinas around the Grand River are sending their contributions to the treasurer of the port authority," I said. The speech lasted about fifteen minutes, followed by questions and answers. I was well received at this meeting. I was glad to give a speech about contributing to the dredging cause. I still had stage fright, but it passed as I continued.

This fishing association made a pledge to help, as I knew they would. This organization was very cooperative. I was a charter member when it was born. Raising money for dredging wasn't a problem with this association.

The same theme was applied to all marinas in the area. W+B Reserve Marina would help carry the ball in favor of funding the project. They could be expected to help in financing, up to a point. They put pressure on the state and federal governments. Some big money people were stepping on the political toes from this organization. They carried some political clout and knew how to flex their political muscle. Their pressure was applied in Columbus.

One evening as Richard was leaving the marina after another brainstorming session, he had another vision. He knew he shouldn't have had that third beer in the marina. Of course Richard couldn't say no to free beer. He turned off the van engine as he saw, *a vision of smoke and fire coming from across the river. The fire is much farther inland and it is over a large area. The dark smoke is rising, spreading over the Mentor Headlands area. I hear fire sirens.*

The Vision of the Mentor Headlands Fire

Richard is struggling to see what is going on. The vision fades from his view. He decides to turn on the radio. He might hear of a fire somewhere. Instead, the radio personality is talking about paranormal phenomena. Richard states, "That's it. I'm having a paranormal phenomenon." Richard says a prayer and heads home.

CHAPTER 15

Evolution of a Cell

Open Door from the North

"Oh, Canada, I will use your country as a springboard to invade the United States of America. Oh, Canada, you are so blind. Please stay that way for a little while longer. Is it your determination to remain so free and open that you will jeopardize your neighbor to the south? We must take advantage of this open border. Thank you very much, Canada. Ohio will be next to feel our venom. Our World Trade Center mission is complete. I am sending another team to America." Captain Awad wrote a passage in his diary.

"We came to this North American continent by freighter. I was on board the old freighter, called the *Gupka*. The executive officer, Lord Barrie, says the *Gupka* has made the Atlantic voyage many times," read this note found on a mangled corpse. Her body was mutilated by a bomb. It was recovered near the scene of a crime in North Perry, Ohio.

Six smuggled-in passengers were kept safe in a secret hold aboard the *Gupka*. The two men are criminals with an unsavory, dangerous past. Abu el Kuri, a Syrian bomber, is an expert in using ordinance. He trained in Afghanistan before it fell from Taliban control. He has done work in Iraq and Egypt. He made car bombs in Iraq and planted bombs at Egyptian tourist sites. Captain Awad recruits him for a North American job. El Kuri is a slippery soul who sneaks into the heart of his targets and gets the most punch from his training. This is what the captain needs.

Saheed Ahmed, an orphan, is a young man taken in by a Muslim imam. The imam helped shape a slanted view of the West for him. He didn't stay long with the imam but found life on the street to his liking. As an orphan, he would steal the shirt off your back. He learned many tricks in how to steal without getting caught. He is street-smart, very detail orientated. He learned how to survive in Iraq. Captain Awad met him in Basra, Iraq. After an on-the-spot interview, Captain Awad asked him to go to Ceyhan, Turkey. The captain waved a nice sum of money at the orphan. He told him to find the freighter *Gupka* and ask for Lord Barrie. Saheed readily complied.

"We have a special mission to do. My leader, Captain Awad, summoned me and my team," said Omma, the eldest woman of the Muslim fighters.

Omma related a story about Captain Awad, while fighting in Soviet Chechnya. Captain Awad was furious when a detonator failed to go off under a Soviet tank. When he returned from battle, I told him I had made a special detonator using a mercury switch. It worked this way. As the tank would come by, the earth would compact and tumble the mercury in the switch. This would start the timer to explode the anti-tank bomb. I demonstrated the device, and he was delighted.

Captain Awad was constantly being called to other lands to organize the fight against the Soviets, the Jews, the West, the infidels. He would say, "We are martyrs and freedom fighters capable of overthrowing governments that oppress the people."

Captain Awad told Omma to be ready to leave this country. Privately he said, "Never share this with anyone. I have a group of store cells planted in America that will prove to all religions that we are the only ones who have the right faith to free our brothers and sisters. We will spread our word across all lands. What we do is right and noble." She believed in him. "Soon, Omma, you will go to America. You will leave your family, friends, and take two of your most trusted soldiers with you," he told me.

The women worked underground in their fight against the Soviet Union. They kept a log book of Soviet troop movements in Chechnya. Omma was handpicked by Captain Awad. She lost her husband and most of her family to a Soviet air raid in Chechnya. She is filled with hatred of the Soviet government and the West. She and her two other handpicked women friends, Hilmah and Camallah, have a mutual story. They lost family members to the Soviets. Their Islamic, extremist upbringing helped cement a radical view of the West.

The information they gathered helped with the Chechnya war effort. By watching the men, they learned military techniques. They were often called upon to repair military hardware. They became semiskilled in working with dynamite and detonators.

They received travel orders and they left by train together. After a long journey through their country, they reached the end of the line. This could also be called the starting point of the next mission. They reached the Turkish port, Ceyhan, where they were given further orders to stowaway on the freighter called *Gupka*. A man called Lord Barrie would help them board.

Two men hide in the Pakistani mountains. They were moved around through Afghanistan because of the war. Somehow, luck was on their side and they stayed one step away from being apprehended or killed. New orders came in for them to take a secret ride in a Turkish freighter bound for North America.

A third young man, Saheed Ahmed, made his way to Turkey by train. He was crafty enough to pretend to be deaf and unable to speak. He helped load baggage for the elderly at the train stations and learned the train routes. Saheed could have paid for his tickets, but chose to do it his way. He eventually got a free ride to Turkey.

They met three women who have similar skills in battle at the Turkish port of Ceyhan, where they boarded the freighter *Gupka*. The men's odyssey included a plane ride to Iran. Both men were given government help to pass across borders. One is an Egyptian, a spiritual leader who will coach fellow Muslims to a new life. Another man is Syrian. All are extremists.

Their common connection was Al-Qaeda member, Captain Awad, the anti-West personality who specializes in terror. Hatred of the West is another common bond. These individuals are trained to use guerilla tactics and cause maximum upheaval. Saheed Ahmed, while not exactly a guerilla freedom fighter, is valuable because of his resourcefulness.

This old maritime freighter has a dual role to play. Role number one, a genuine shipment of textiles is being delivered. The second role for the ship is a very profitable one, a smuggling business. The owner of the freighter is a company that can be traced back to Turkey. Lions Goods International is the company that owns the *Gupka*. They have three freighters. One freighter works the Pacific Rim. The second one moves back and forth from West Africa to South America. A third ship is used to transport merchandise from Europe to North America. The *Gupka* works the Atlantic Ocean and Mediterranean Sea. A flag flies from the *Gupka* which has a Lion embroidered on it. This ship has a mixture of Egyptian, Libyan, and Moroccan sailors who make up the crew. They have worked together for years. They are a salty group of worn and seasoned seafarers who are on board the *Gupka* because of their special skills in handling this old freighter. They can make the big money and command a respect for the illegal mission they play on the high seas. This ship does not command any special attention as it comes into ports. It simply has the poor boy look. The average onlooker would look the other way when this ship comes into the harbor. Because of this non-headliner look, it serves a special mission. The *Gupka* will carry a malicious cargo, terrorist stowaways. The men will form one cell and the women another.

The English-speaking man, Lord Barrie, is coming into your country. The gifted Executive Officer is offered to the customs inspectors as the ship's ambassador. He was educated in a British university. He is a diplomat's son from Morocco. He has such a way with words that most custom agents give his ship a free pass into port. He will plead mercy for his crew. The executive officer says to the customs agents that his ship is over worked. It is plain to see they are a poor shipping liner looking to be saved by Canada. They need Canada and its safe harbor. Their ship is in need of repairs. They battled a perilous storm. Give them shelter for they cannot sail much longer.

The customs agents don't even want to be aboard the scow. The deck is littered with miscellaneous drums and cargo shifted from an organized state to a bungled mess. Rags have been used to clean up spills. Many of these are discarded here and there. Merchandise in crates is broken open, exposing rugs and tapestry. The ship has obviously been deranged by a storm. All of this staged acting sets in motion another plan. Customs gave the *Gupka* a quick look and then sent the ship to a safe mooring site to receive a repair crew. The EX officer received a standing ovation from the crew.

After the ship is finally tied up, an exchange takes place. A financial agent with two rather strong-arm gentlemen is looking on. A large briefcase is given to the ship's captain in the captain's quarters. Not much is said as this payoff takes place. As the old navy expression goes, "loose lips sink ships." The financial agent and his bodyguards leave the ship. This whole operation takes only a few minutes.

The captain now gives the EX the crew's pay. The executive officer has the crew form a line. Soon a tidy sum of cash is dispensed to the crew as a reward for their voyage and silence. Again, there is very little talk. They know that the money they receive is excellent pay.

Stowaways are a cash commodity. This voyage must have been special because the captain has included an extra stipend. "Go ashore and be back within twenty-four hours," he says. "I'm sure our next adventure will be equally rewarding." The captain and executive officers return to the captain's quarters. The captain puts a large amount of cash into the ships safe. The officers cut of the pie is tied by a customary red silk ribbon. The red ribbon denotes the shares allotted to the two main officers. Also, inside the briefcase is a laptop computer with the captain's initials engraved on the outside. His password was given to him when they were in Turkey. Instructions on the laptop provide for the next movement of the ship.

The captain types in his password. The two commanding officers examine the future movement of the old freighter. It has a Lake Erie adventure in its sail. The instructions say, "When the repairs to the ship are complete, your ship needs to be prepared to make a number of pickups of passengers. On June 27, make off shore pickups in Buffalo and Toledo. Wait outside the three-mile mark, as your ship will be visited. There you will have new crew members that need to be taken on board. They will only be with you one day. On June 28, these new people will be transferred to yachts at night. After this you will sail north and then east. You will remain at sea until July 4. That evening, you will be off the eastern Ohio mainland near Madison's Arcola Creek and will wait for a signal. Members of a cell will be rowing a boat out from shore. Around 8:00 PM to 9:00 PM an enormous eruption will take place west of your location. This will signal your need to get to the drop zone. Sail back to the Canadian marina where you will wait to pick up yachts arriving from southern Lake Erie. This will happen on July 5. Be in place near the Canadian marina about 4:00 AM. Several yachts will join you. The crew of these yachts will need to be taken to Buffalo, New York."

A maintenance group arrived to help the *Gupka*. These Middle-Eastern men, called land crabs, came aboard. They are called this because their service is rarely used way out at sea. They hug the shore not willing to be away from home for long stretches. They are a ship's repairmen called in to fix broken machinery. This professional maintenance crew is dressed alike. Their blue overalls are well maintained. On the uniform a stencil is stamped with the company name, Victory Company. A lion is carrying the letter V in his mouth which gives the uniform class. This is another front company designed to do double duty. They bring six extra uniforms onto the ship. Our six stowaways are seemingly hired into the repair crew and given blue coveralls. They work with the others until the end of the day. They don't communicate very well. The foreman manages the situation until the end of the work day. Most everyone leaves the ship to be picked up by prearranged transportation. However, our stowaways, after debarking from the ship, are picked up in a white Victory

Company construction van. Their next stop will be at a large Canadian marina. Again under the disguise of maintenance workers, they board a tug boat. There, another change of clothes is waiting. Soon they are transferred to a thirty-six foot yacht that takes them to the shores of Northern Ohio. They off load in Fairport Harbor and another van ride take them to a remote safe house. They can now unwind continuing to stay out of the limelight.

The evolution of this cell started months ago. The people buying into the extremist portion of the faith don't see themselves coming together into a cell until the last part of the plan is put into motion. This idea has certain security strengths. Action dates are born very fast. Quickness keeps any weak link from backing out. A weakness in this theory is a lack of final preparation. No rehearsals can mean trouble. However, the rapid development of this plan is needed to prevent the FBI from being tipped off by insiders that have lost their way. When something goes wrong with an exit plan, they sometimes have to shoot it out. This is the way the soldiers are trained. Evidence of this can be seen from the battles in Saudi Arabia and Pakistan.

Supercell leaders are collecting a dossier of information on the strengths of individuals. New inductees may have some personal experience, expertise, and training in handling weapons, ordinance, or lingual skills. Special battle skills will earn a special job. The suicide martyr will wear a bomber's vest. Such devotion to the cause will earn the surviving family members a monetary payment. A merit is earned when a potential cell member stays in training long enough to earn a trust award. Mr. Big will give permission to wear the lion medallion, the lion ring, or bracelet. A lion is used as the symbol of trust. A final dose of head training is included to make sure potential cell member have focus on the spiritual end game. An imam refreshes the recruit with inspiring words that include giving up one's life. This constant guidance keeps the recruits acquainted with death and reward. Some parallel can be drawn as Japan was being routed in World War II. Japan assembled suicide pilots to make a final sacrifice.

CHAPTER 16

❀

Cell Trouble

Great care must be taken now. Some of our brothers have been taken down in Canada. "Our cells are not being careful." Bin Laden complains. Canada and America will increase security along the northern border.

The two countries didn't look like they could remedy this open border. They were Siamese countries that were joined at the back of their heads. Each was looking away from the other was the best way to explain their mutual misunderstanding.

Today each government is waking up. This is very disturbing to Bin Laden and his planted cells.

"I have sent the orders out using the Arabian News and al Jazeera. The Internet is helping with our codes. Supercell leaders will decode messages using arranged food stores. Computer communications was being used more and more. Attack the enemy worldwide has been ordered. Remaining Canadian cell members are being teamed at the Toronto stores and will hide until Captain Awad orders them to America," Bin Laden's words carried on ominous tone, because he received more bad news.

Bin Laden's chief in Iraq, Abu Musab Al-Zarqawi, was killed. The air strike that took him out was another blow to Al-Qaeda in Iraq. This new development brings mounting pressure on Bin Laden. He has lost another deputy in his fight to spread the Al—Qaeda word. Bin Laden lost a symbol of strength in Iraq. Zarqawi acted as if he was invincible. This loss proves to the Iraqi people that Al-Qaeda is actually vulnerable. Bin Laden was somewhat concerned about the work of Zarqawi. The Zarqawi image was overshadowing the name of Bin Laden.

Our American operation is funded. Big Man is at the site. He will execute the plan at the Independence Day Mardi Gras. When Mr. Big commands, we attack." Bin Laden finishes his brief meeting with his personal messenger.

Bin Laden tells the messenger to report to operatives in Washington, DC.

CHAPTER 17

Recruitment

I believe a terrorist is a soldier who is alone and unhappy with life. He or she resents people who are doing well. They scornfully look at the West with its wealth and relative social calm. This must make them easy recruits to try and undermine our very existence. Why would anyone decide they should blow themselves up? If it were just a matter of dooming oneself, that would be called suicide. Taking a few unsuspecting so-called enemies of Islam in the name of some extremist ideology makes the course of action justifiable. I say what is residing inside of you is that tarnished, brainwashed mind. The spiritual leaders have provided you with reasons to start all over in another world. So go and bomb an unbeliever. This will be your key to heaven. This is going to solve a religious matter. They must impose their correct version of Islam into the West.

They work for months understanding American style. They received ample spiritual training which burns hatred in their hearts. I see a common theme rattled off daily. They believe Americans are the crusaders. Imams demand the recruits avenge all the evil in Israel and the United States. It is America's fault. Their land has been taken. Their brothers are being killed by the infidels. It is this continuous chorus that is preached to the younger Arabs. A good example is the terrorist that is the president of Iran. Mahmoud Ahmadinejad was one of the participants in the kidnapping of the U.S. Embassy staff in Iran. That was a long time ago. Mr. Ahmadinejad didn't turn in his terrorist inclinations. To this day, he would really like to wipe Israel off the face of the map. He wasn't born a terrorist. Innocent children are transformed, educated, and indoctrinated to become terrorists. Enough hatred is conjured up in the recruits that they become ready to take a final exam. Unfortunately, the one-way exam is truly a last visit with life on earth. Having only one shot to fire is enough. Death is not an ending, but what the imams call a journey to heaven. The imam is never a passenger.

This reward system is talked up over and over. The young girl or boy doesn't have the opportunity to weigh any other choice. Eternal life for the guys with a choice of fair maidens is too much to pass up. A Palestinian girl in Israel was caught with a bomber's vest on. Asked why she was going to blow herself up at a hospital, she told this story. She was disfigured because of an accident. She was unhappy being disfigured and probably wouldn't marry, so she might as well take out a few Jews. Israeli doctors were trying to help her mend. She was offered money which would be paid to her family when she blows herself up. Fortunately, she was caught before she returned to the hospital. She was going to kill the doctors that were trying to help her. The twisted minds cannot live in a normal society. Saddam Hussein, former leader in Iraq, offered money as bounty for a family member who would blow himself up in Israel. The bomber could never achieve this wealth in their current jobless state. While jobless, young recruits are easy prey, led to a death trap.

So far they have reached America once. I find the idea of a terrorist cell here is tough to comprehend. I don't want to follow my dreams.

CHAPTER 18

Valuable Targets

Messages are sent out from Osama Bin Laden that an urgent shift in the timeline is needed. Iraq has become a lost cause. The Iraqi people have turned against the rebel movement. They have voted in a government. Reluctantly, Sunni Arabs are joining Shiites and Kurds in the democratic process. Al-Qaeda in Iraq is causing losses without enough return. Iraqi insurgent fighters are defecting to the Iraqi government. More bad news, Al-Qaeda members are being rounded up in Saudi Arabia and haven't disrupted world oil supplies enough to cause a crisis. It is of great importance to open a new front. "We must show some battlefield victories so our religious movement retains freedom fighters," said Bin Laden in the message. His loss of a key supercell leader in Pakistan and Saudi Arabia is hurting morale among Al-Qaeda ranks.

Interpol, the international police organization, was actively pursuing Al-Qaeda cell members in Europe. Bin Laden must pin down these investigators. Bin Laden would use some bombings in Egypt and Saudi Arabia to keep pressure on these governments. That would tie up Interpol investigators.

Supercell leaders should activate the American-Canadian plan. The coded message was clearly outlined for Mr. Big and Captain Awad. The North American units will be committed for battle. It was up to Al-Qaeda in North America to show his world forces that Al-Qaeda is alive and well. The Great Lakes Basin, where Osama Bin Laden's forces are forming, is now an active front. The long-range plan is being moved to the front burner. The Arab Internet contained codes for Mr. Big. His associate leaders, Captain Awad and Lord Barrie would read the same message. "Active Canada, marine, store Ohio123 is planted now growing." Inside Internet phrases was the message: "Planted sleeper cells will awake immediately. Supercell leaders ready your members."

Some codes are sent through blogs by Internet and newspapers ads. World supercell leaders are seeing encrypted messages. Egyptian supercell leaders activate a tourist bombing and a mysterious accident on a ship carrying hundreds of workers. "Cairo, Egypt activates." Captain Awad is referenced. Advertising trips to Ohio and Ontario is meant to convey a message to the supercells, meaning, Canada cells are to awake. Ohio cells are to awake. "Contacts must converge, Captain Awad." The Captain Awad message continues, "Vital tourist sites are to be examined. You may start your local plan now. Go Great Lakes." Quickly, supercell leaders are devising a local master plan.

Local Plan A

Late at night inside a food store office, leaders discuss plans of action. Mr. Big and Captain Awad are leading this meeting. Supercell store owners are in attendance along with Omma, Hilmah, and Camallah. The three ladies were invited to shore up their part of the mission.

The terrorists needed to tie up the security and emergency forces so that they could maximize the killing and mayhem. Several plans were floated around. A plan to blow bridges across main highways crossing the Grand River along the interstate highway in Ohio was kicked around. This soft target wouldn't achieve a dramatic effect. It is not significant enough for Mr. Big. The Cleveland sports event would be a nice target, but carry many security problems. This plan was dropped. One beauty was to topple a communication tower situated on a main road going into Grand River. Included in the plan was to create a series of fires about the Mentor and Grand River nature preserves. The Mentor marsh is a likely target. Every so often the marsh catches fire so it won't raise the specter of greater pending disaster. This diversion could easily be fomented by the women. These trained experts are well-conditioned women in their late twenties. They have been battle tested in the Soviet Chechnya conflict. Our fire starter team will consist of Omma, Hilmah, and Camallah. The commanders are a bit apprehensive, especially the women's captain, Awad. Captain Awad works with all newcomers.

Captain Awad does his best to hide the fact that he had an affair with Omma. He doesn't want the other two women to know. He's still in love with her and must keep his mind straight. Back in Chechnya, they worked together and developed a fond relationship after Omma lost her husband. Captain Awad does his best to conceal his affection for her.

He says, "If the women have to address someone this would give attention to their lack of command of the language. The women have done well to remain out of the limelight since sneaking into the country across Lake Erie. Their appearance will need to be altered. They look too much like Soviets. "Hilmah wears her ruby earrings all the time. Omma's makeup and hairdo gives into Soviet style. Camallah has a Soviet hair cover that's not right. I sometimes have difficulty teaching our women the Western ways of life. This may give the infidels a source of concern. These women haven't been in the country long enough to escape the scrutiny of someone in America." The captain is quick to recall the look of that old woman in the Grand River restaurant. "A few weeks ago when we were testing our women in moving about the citizenry, there was an incident at the restaurant. At the time, a patron of the restaurant gave the women a good look over. There is something uncanny about that old lady. She seems to know something about our women. I could see her observing us. She wasn't completely interested in our party, but I think our women gave her reason to become suspicious. I'm not completely sold on giving this assignment to the women." Captain Awad knows how dangerous their job will be. Deep down, he is protecting his love.

Captain Awad is the coordinator. Running agents across the lake is part of his duties. Captain Awad would continue to wonder about the ladies' assignment after he was overruled by Mr. Big. "Are the ladies up to this task? Sure these women are battle tested. They need a man with them. They will obey, but my doubt has me worried." What Captain Awad didn't say was he wanted to go with the women as their protector. Captain Awad needed more time to prepare the women.

"I have heard excuses, not answers. The women will do the job," Mr. Big exclaimed. Captain Awad is overruled. The women shall be involved as time is running down. Mr. Big, the senior leader, has made his call.

"The women will be their own decision makers. Here is the plan. Quiet and without notice is a requirement to achieve the objective. The part the women will play is secondary, but it will enhance the master plan even if their work becomes unhinged. We know they could hold off half an army. Their mission is to be a menace to rescue services. Stealth and courage is a requirement to achieve their objective." Mr. Big explains all this as he provides a little pep talk.

Captain Awad says, "They would set up and operate a mortar placement and send multiple smoke and incendiary charges into the wildlife refuge in the western marsh near Grand River. I have shown the women placements and targets of interest. I outlined the directions with Omma when we dined at the restaurant. She will lead. Omma can pick and choose how many targets to be ignited. Their way in and out of town has been considered. She will make a decision to go to the secondary targets after sending multiple salvos into the surrounding marsh and forest. Next, they can snap the cell-phone tower as they exit Grand River. The Painesville and Grand River cell-phone tower will fall with base charges. This will block a main road back to Fairport Harbor. That will be a plus. Correctly placed, the tower might fall far enough over the Fairport Harbor to Grand River's Richmond Street. This will seal off the firefighters from responding to our Mardi Gras bomb fire.'" Trying to add humor, Captain Awad says, "Let's call it the 'marsh.com@Mardi party fire." The group has a good laugh as they toast each other with cups of tea. The captain adds, "This cell phone tower will not affect our cell phones. I have checked the communication maps. It is not part of our system."

Omma and the other women study the maps of primary roads. The women agree that a couple remote controlled dynamite charges on the base of the communication tower will bring it down. This part of the mission could be set in motion prior to advancing to the marsh. Omma states, "Once the marsh is primed, we will drive by the communication tower and press the detonation device. We will then head east on Route 20. We will drive to Antiock Road in Perry. The road leading to the Perry Nuclear Plant property is close by. Here is where we may have problems." Captain Awad adds, "Omma, you may find it necessary to review your timeline here. If you are ahead of schedule, you could stop at a restaurant or a park nearby. There are plenty of places near Antiock Road where you could decide the next step. The baseball fields along the lake are not far from the power plant. That would be an excellent place to hide."

Captain Awad has done some homework on the Perry nuke site. He says, "The Perry Nuclear Power Plant has a perimeter fence. It has surveillance cameras. The random fence check of the cameras will permit the women enough time to set up and fire three times at the security personnel and their headquarters. They will locate a new position for lobbing three or more mortar salvos into the control buildings. They must make a quick exit. By using the back of the truck as their mobile launcher pad, they can exit quickly and head east again using the back roads until they come to Dock Road. Omma, drive north to the end of Dock Road. Your team will take a boat from the scene and row until the team is picked up by watercraft off Madison's Dock Road. Our extraction boat, a thirty-foot yacht, will recover the team. You row from shore exactly at 10:00 PM. The timeline properly carried out will be: Grand River mission at 6:20 PM, topple the communication tower at 6:35 PM. The power plant burst will commence at 8:20 PM with extraction as said. A fresh auto with clothes in the trunk will be parked on the end of Dock Road. If the extraction team does not arrive by 10:20 PM, the women will drive to Chautauqua, New York. Two glove box phones will provide details should this be needed. A small row boat will be on top of the auto. Use the key pad on the door to gain access. The code is 686868."

Mr. Big speaks, "The nuclear power plant was going to be the primary target. That has changed. The American crusaders and Jews will never expect the Mardi Gras bombing along with the Grand River operation. Our survey cell has checked the waters around the Perry power plant, and the survey revealed a lower reward. We know the power plant would shut down before any serious contamination would be released. Also they are watching the waters north of the plant. We will scrap this idea. A knockout blow which will release radioactive contamination would require more assets than we can provide. We have found some information out through a small test of their security. The Perry nuclear site is a tough nut to crack. Only a limited operation is planned for Perry as we outlined with the ladies. A suicide plane was considered to crash into the control center. Again, this idea was scrapped because the plant will just shutdown with no real damage to the surrounding areas. A diver team was going to blow the water intake. They would draw immediate attention and the team would probably be caught before any damaging charges could be set. It is decided to use our men for our sapper cell and our suicide bombers will be men. They will work in Fairport Harbor. The salt mine has become a priority target. I will hold the details of that operation for later."

CHAPTER 19

✣

Terrorist Cargo via Lake Erie

Lake Erie has many a foreign traveler. The ocean shippers come from around the world. The ocean-going ships eventually get into Lake Erie. They enter the Saint Lawrence Seaway and pass through the locks near Niagara Falls. Called the Welland Canal, I watched the system of locks move ships along from Lake Erie to Lake Ontario. During the shipping season vessels of all sizes are crisscrossing the Great Lakes.

Because Cleveland is an international port, it is natural for vessels of different nationalities to come calling at this port. Most of the freighters have routine duty. Delivering cargo and picking up goods is normal.

Some of these vessels have crew members of dubious backgrounds on board. A maritime sailor with criminal intentions can pick up some extra cash exchanging contraband items. A ship may carry erroneously marked merchandise which is to be off loaded in a special way. One such ship is a Liberian registered freighter called the *Istanbul El V*. It had frozen fish on board. It would stop in Cleveland and make a delivery. Although that isn't abnormal, a curious exchange takes place along the way.

Mr. Piraye, Captain of the *El V* met a gentleman in Cleveland who is a representative of the port authority in Cleveland. His name is Mr. Columbo. "I have a special payment to make to you, Mr. Piraye," Mr. Columbo explains. "Tonight, after you leave the Cleveland harbor, you need to drop off some burlap sacks to a yacht that will be following you." Mr. Columbo hands Mr. Piraye an envelope. "This advance payment is for carrying and delivery of extra cargo that is being loaded on your ship. Also inside, you will find instructions and a phone number to call as you near Fairport Harbor. We received this shipment from Buffalo, New York. I don't want to use the highway to Fairport Harbor from here. The goods are too special to travel in traffic or risk a nighttime problem with the law. The police around Euclid, Willoughby, and Mentor are on their toes. I feel better about a nighttime drop from a ship." Mr. Piraye feels the bills in the envelope. "Mr. Columbo this envelope should help cover the transportation costs," says Mr. Piraye.

Mr. Piraye, former captain of the *Gupka*, was no saint. He was called the "Pirate of the Salties." He earned this nickname for stealing oil from Nigeria in the nineties. His Mediterranean Sea adventures in Nigeria were never equaled. He would off load thousands of barrels of oil that he bought at a bargain price from the locals in Nigeria. Buyers in Sicily were pleased with Mr. Piraye's reasonably priced crude. He needed a change in scenery so he took the job as skipper of the *Istanbul El V*. This scalawag Mr. Piraye and another, Mr. Yilmaz, always found moneymaking schemes in the shipping business.

During the night, the crew member of ill repute, a Turkish man named Baki Yilmaz, was assigned another duty by the captain. Baki Yilmaz was hired by Captain Piraye to do a special job. The captain paid Baki in cash to handle a late-night drop.

Baki would dump black burlap sacks overboard after receiving a special command. An interceptor craft called the *thirty-sixer* would be in the right place to do some burlap sack fishing. The men on board the interceptor craft would tail the freighter with their lights off. Saheed Ahmed, on board the pick up yacht, would operate a cell phone. His cell phone text messages would aid in the timing of the elicit exchange. A message would be sent to Baki. After they exchange identities, they advance into the main operation. "Prepare for a drop, Baki, we are behind you." Baki would see the message on his cell phone. "Baki, drop sacks A, B, and C." An amber beacon is on sack A. Blue beacon is on sack B and a white beacon is on sack C. The lights wouldn't go on right away. The lake water activated the beacons on the sacks after a couple minutes in the water.

The crews on the *thirty-sixer* are not perfect sailors. They have been trained for land jobs and this work is tough on the lake. This is especially true when Lake Erie kicks up as a northeastern wind grows intense. The skipper has enough talent. His first mate has been around but the others are new arrivals and need to grow some sea legs. The lake is rearing its head tonight as the rendezvous takes place. The exchanged goods are bouncing about in the water. *Thirty-sixer*'s captain has made several passes to help the crew rescue a sack of supplies. The collaborators would have carried out the mission this night almost flawlessly if it wasn't for Lake Erie and its dangerous storms. It's the "B" sack that had been dropped from the *El V* that was proving to be a difficult pickup in the rolling waves. The hook untied the drawstring opening the burlap sack. The plastic bags were about to release from the sack. The sailors finally got lucky, and all of the contents were brought aboard. "This sack is a little loose," says Saheed Ahmed. He thinks something is missing. The others say everything is fine. They don't think any goods have escaped. They just want to get on land.

The "B" sack contained dynamite.

The *thirty-sixer* takes the burlap sacks to the Fairport Harbor Port Authority boat ramp. Abu el Kuri remarks, "No one is here tonight. This is perfect." Captain Awad arrives in a white van and he loads the goods to take to the food stores. This delivery was important because it contained a large load of dynamite, remote controls, bomber belts, and cash. Captain Awad was very worried the extra mortar tube and shells wouldn't make it. They are in the shipment. They didn't receive the X device. "Kuri, did you loose any dynamite? The sack is open." Asks Captain Awad. "No, Sir," answers Abu el Kuri.

The *thirty-sixer* has made trips to the Canadian marina for supplies of ammunition off loading to smaller fishing boats which sail on to Fairport Harbor. Captain Awad makes sure that deliveries are made in the evening at the port authority courtesy dock. Sometimes the small fishing boats would sail up the river to the small boat ramp at the big tent construction site. Some goods are moved upriver where they are handed off at the old Diamond Shamrock bulkhead. This remote area won't attract much attention. These special deliveries are then moved on to the food stores where the supercell managers take charge of the goods. The special nature of the contents makes this part of the mission so important. A supercell leader is always keeping close tabs on the goods. These packages need to be put in safe keeping. An inventory of the goods is kept safely locked away.

One day a yacht has pulled up on the far side of the river and tie off along the bulkhead. Instantly, a white van appears. Some sort of transfer is taking place across from Mary Ann's boat ramp. She strains her eyes to see who has grabbed her attention. Even though it is getting dark, she can make out the silhouettes of the people. She can hear the voices of the workers. She remembers seeing that boat. The telling sign that caught her eyes is the way they have tied up the boat. She is filled with uneasiness. She goes inside her office to grab a pen and paper. The men make a quick exchange off loading the cargo into a white van. The boat pulls away as she tries to write down the boat's license number. She's not fast enough to write down everything although she remembers the first couple of numbers. The van speeds away along the dirt road. Mary Ann doesn't want to jump to conclusions but she's seen enough right now to burn this to memory.

CHAPTER 20

The Attack Plan

The basement at the Painesville store is set up with nice chairs and a large table to accommodate the supercell leaders. This particular meeting has an air of high importance. The room is clean. It is decorated with flowers. Two stainless-steel tea pots are situated with cups in one corner of the room. A lieutenant at the door upstairs keeps a close vigil this late night. The chauvinistic Mr. Big is the headmaster of the meeting. He will have the final say. Captain Awad is coordinator of the cell members and organizer of attack plans. Mr. Big is dressed in a light blue business suit. Captain Awad has on his leisure suit reflective of the warm weather. The map on the wall, unveiled by Captain Awad, call out specific targets that will be featured in the attack. It is by far the most detailed presentation so far. Supercell leaders who are store owners can see exactly which cell member they will be supplying.

Mr. Big opens by saying. "Gentlemen focus your attention on me. What I say is what we do. This meeting is not an open discussion. It is the plan."

Mr. Big speaks. "The last day of the Mardi Gras will feature fireworks around 9:00 PM. The Fairport Harbor festival will be loaded with party revelers. With all those people assembled, waiting for the fireworks, we will have the most opportune time to hatch the master plan. Right before the first *boom* of the fireworks display, our boom goes off and we will strike in many directions. The distracter cell, which Omma is leading, will already have struck a blow in the neighboring town. Their work will tie up safety and security forces. This diversion by the women will allow us to sneak other cells into prearranged places. We will set up a surprise attack on the land-based lighthouse in Fairport Harbor. We will overtake the operators at the lighthouse. Our men will go to the top with weapons and ammunition. Our three-member team will set up a machine gun placement overlooking both the entrance and the main escape route from the Mardi Gras. High Street will be used as the main exit for the Mardi Gras patrons. When the mortar rounds start to explode on the midway the people will panic. Then we will riddle retreating patrons with machine-gun fire from atop the lighthouse. Security forces can be pinned down by the use of a single sniper on the south side of the lighthouse. This force will be in and out of the tower in a matter of ten to fifteen minutes.

"On the lakefront a double yacht flotilla will be busy lobbing in mortar rounds as two young suicide bombers fire bomb the sheriff's trailer that is parked on the grounds of the Mardi Gras. One bomber will forcibly enter the trailer without any warning. The other bomber will be stationed by the rear door to completely eliminate their communications site. The precision timing of our events will cause such mayhem we will be able to swiftly exit. Our ground forces will retreat by running to the port authority boat ramp. The yachts will pick up our heroic lighthouse tower fighters. Be very fast in your retreat. We will wait only five minutes at the ramp. About 9:35, the yachts will leave. One yacht will go east to Dock Road in Madison and pick up the female fighters. The other yacht shall return to our Canadian marina. All boats will return to Canada and everyone will transfer to the freighter *Gupka*."

Mr. Big paces the floor as he continues. "The *thirty-sixer* will be downriver. Two plans have been developed for downriver. One team of sappers will carry timer controlled dynamite charges. This cell will descend to the bottom of the salt company shaft and set charges alongside the support columns. They can start their operation about 8:15 PM. They will be out of the shaft by 9:15 PM and explode the charges within that hour. I will detonate a super bomb made from fertilizer and chemical mix in the base camp shaft. This timed boom will happen sometime after he picks up the sappers that lay the charges in the mine. Since we have excavated the shaft to 200 feet deep, I anticipate this will cause a break in the underground mine all the way up to the Grand River. As that happens, the Grand River will start to flow into the salt mine. This action might cause a roiling river water action overwhelming the boat traffic in the area. The *thirty-sixer* will have picked up our salt mine sapper cell. We all make a controlled dash to the lake. As the *thirty-sixer* passes the coast guard station, we will fire grenade launcher rockets into the station and any rescue boats at the dock. We will travel out to the open lake and watch the smaller yachts destroy the Mardi Gras midway by mortar explosions. Any attempt made to interfere with the mortar team will be met by the *thirty-sixer*. The *thirty-sixer* will be the last craft to Canada. Do not take any prisoners. Cell phones are provided to extract anyone left behind. There is an emergency number in the phone directory to let you know how to proceed. Call this number and a message will be sent back to you. It will tell you how to proceed. The phones will be given to each supercell leader at the end of this meeting. Do not use these phones at any time unless you are in danger of being left behind. You will distribute them to the cell members. Keep your cell phones on you when the mission starts."

Mr. Big does not leave behind living cell members. If a cell member gets lost on the battlefield, the cell phone will solve the problem. Should any member of Mr. Big's mission call the directory emergency phone number a message will appear saying, "Good-bye." The cell phone's battery will then explode.

Mr. Big pontificates, "The local crusaders and Jews can read about the experience from the *Lake County Voice* newspaper. I will mail the newspaper an ad. It will describe our jihad three days after the sting. I will tell them what they must do next or face another example. Our vision for America and our version of the truth will be realized. All the Americans will need to convert to our religion."

CHAPTER 21

❀

U.S. Operations

Richard saw an important update on the news regarding port security. It was under consideration that the large ports in New Jersey, New York, and other states would be run by an Arab owned company. This caused a furor with the American people and Congress. Thinking of the problems this backlash presented, it was shot down by the government in the United Arab Emirates. Richard was motivated by this update. He decides he will speak to the FBI.

He went to the Cleveland FBI headquarters and was eventually directed to Agent Ron Roman.

Agent Ron Roman, an Iowa University graduate, had been a heavyweight wrestling champion at the university. He gained a few pounds since his wrestling days.

Mr. Roman was familiar with Fairport Harbor and Grand River. He fished there, which was a special reason he paid attention to Richard's concern. "I launch my fishing boat at Mary Ann Rutherford's boat launch," Ron said. "Everyone knows Mrs. Rutherford," I said. "Agent Roman, I'm not a crackpot. I'm a concerned citizen who feels the port security is not up to speed in Fairport Harbor. I have a suspicion that an undesirable element is moving into our area, namely terrorists. I see more and more foreign faces around the town. Agent Roman, is there anything being done to address the security issues of small ports in America? Do we check people coming into the harbor?" I asked.

"The ports and borders around America are receiving greater attention. Obviously the bigger cities will receive greater scrutiny. All the Homeland Security departments are working to root out the bad guys. We have many illegals in this country. Most illegal's are employed and working to secure their family's future. While it is difficult to secure all areas in this country, we do monitor high value places, most border crossings, and ports." He said, "Rest assured, we check many foreign nationals each day. You have to remember many visitors to the United States are here legally. They are not terrorists. Your generalization about foreigners is not accurate. We appreciate your concern and thanks for keeping a watch on my fishing hole. I landed some nice walleye off Fairport Harbor." He wrote a few notes and escorted me to the elevator.

I wasn't sure if this trip paid off, but I did get to speak with a real agent. I thought that was pretty cool. "If Agent Roman got a hold of a bad guy, he'd have a hard time getting away. That man was a big dude. His hands were twice the size of mine," I said to myself.

Agent Roman made a call to the CIA headquarters in Virginia. He spoke to a section chief about terrorist activity around the northern part of Ohio, Pennsylvania, and New York. The section chief said he would check into any recent action in the area. His staff assigned to this area was reviewing their data all the time.

At the CIA headquarters, some members were busy deciphering messages from Al-Qaeda. They know it has been busy in Europe the past year. Turkey, Spain, and Britain have been hit. The reach of the terrorists is covering most of several continents. North America has natural high-value targets which they would like to ruin. Since 9/11, plots here and there have been discovered and vanquished. Some of these unfriendly perpetrators have been sent back to their homelands when there wasn't enough evidence to convict in a court of law. One member of the 9/11 plot is on trail. Others are in prison or awaiting judicial action. We are concerned about the ones who are under the radar. This is one reason we have deployed a number of task forces to circumvent their evil plans. New York City and Los Angeles are prime cities where mass casualties could occur with a biological or chemical weapon. We have people working inside these cities to prevent this. The terrorist has to get into the country first before he can do damage. Our main entry points are receiving top security coverage. We have a number of small groups training to understand the medium risk targets. They check borders, airports, harbors, and seaports that haven't received the attention the big ones have. Since there is such a wide range of ways into the country, we have to rely on the local citizens, police, and our own Homeland Security units for help in identifying the bad guys to some degree. This layered security plan can work.

The latest Internet chatter was of importance in that a few people, who are agents of Iran and Syria, were chatting about some water event that was coming. The CIA decipherers perused the steady stream of talk, looking for a hidden sign. They wanted to see some group of words or lyrics in a song which could be tagged for immediate scrutiny. The computers would help translate foreign language. A trail or a tag is put on words that may have meaning about targets inside the United States. This trail is delivered to another computer that references special tagged words or phrases, all of which would then be worked up for possible meaning. In the end, the decipherers would find a best of best lead to follow. A town, state, or country might be identified. This chase could end with an undercover person going out to do a field examination. A drone might be used to fly over a zone of interest.

Two ladies with experience around Lake Erie and Lake Ontario are assigned to research border data. Karen is from the Buffalo, New York area and Charlotte is from a small town east of Cleveland, Ohio. They are part of the decipher team.

Charlotte says, "The messages today seem to say some potential target might be over water, a cruise ship, something like that." So far the two women working the computers crunched that much out of the latest data. A freighter is somehow connected to a plan in progress. They think a boat or ship will be the target. Karen asks, "What about the ocean liners out of Florida or New York. The port cities of San Francisco or Long Beach, could they be a target?" She adds, "We have so many ports to cover just on the Great Lakes. It might take a month to decide where we should be looking. Remember, they gave us a black eye over the USS *Cole*." The section leader asks the ladies to code in the Great Lakes Basin. "Let's sweep that area one time. The FBI took down a terrorist cell in Buffalo, New York. There may be another cell around. Check for a Canadian tie," he says. The CIA has teams of workers trying to figure out what Al-Qaeda is planning to do next.

CHAPTER 22

Disturbing Information

I noticed I had a message on my answering machine. I pressed the button and listened. "This is Mia Booker from Painesville Township. I would like you to take pictures of our church league's youth softball team. I'm the manager of the Painesville Raiders. I saw your advertisement in the church flyer when we were at church Sunday. Please call me."

She left her phone number and address. I was so happy my ad caught somebody's eye. "Richard Stern, Action Shots are my photography specialty," was how I listed the ad. Father Pete told me I should put an ad in the church flyer. He was right about it attracting business. Hey, for ten bucks it did the job. This was a break for me. Baseball and softball are big summertime sports around here. I felt like my photography business was about to lift off. I called her back. "Hello, Mrs. Booker, this is Richard Stern, the photographer. I'm kicking off, or should I say, taking a swing at, the next photo ops season. You're going to get a great deal being my first softball team to photograph this season. How about if I stop by your house and I'll show you some of my past photos?" She agreed. She was happy I could come by right away.

I only had a fair amount of photos of my son's baseball team from a couple of years back but I felt that I could sell my work with what photos I had. This photo album would act as my business display. My son played on a great high school team and I took some really nice shots of their winning ways. I framed the very good pictures and put the work inside a briefcase. It was time to market my business.

I arrived at Mrs. Booker's house about noon. Her house was across the street from the recreational park where the baseball fields were located. This was really an ideal setup—my customer right next to the ball fields. I laid out a spread of pictures and gave her a few different price ranges. She agreed to use my low—budget program. "I'll pay for your time taking the group pictures myself. If parents want more diverse photos, they could contract with you directly," she said. That was fine with me; I got my foot in the door.

The fields are located three hundred or so feet from a steep drop to the lake. There is a grassy area and parking in front of the bank leading down to the water. A few paths have been made that will permit a person to descend to the lake. It is not an easy access to the lake and you have to be in good shape to climb back up. The view is breathtaking as you can see Fairport Harbor and the lighthouse from the bank. About three or four miles out you can see lake freighters moving across Lake Erie. I remarked how peaceful this place is before baseball season. "You're so fortunate to have a house next to the lake bank," I said. When I said that, I saw her wince. Her tone became cautionary. She told me an interesting story about something that happened recently that upset her.

"Our neighborhood is full of kids who naturally team together. These boys and girls stick together. They aren't what you would call a gang. They could be called the Painesville Township youth patrol. They are like a team in sports. It's a diverse group, Hispanic, French, and American, between ten and fifteen years old. They are the modern-day technolecents. Some have cell phones. They are a circle of the same friends that run around the neighborhood like most modern-day adventurers. You recognize who some kids are by the color of their cell phone and the backpack they carry."

"Well, Mr. Stern, the kids found a bomb by the shore right over the bank," she said. She pointed to an area near the ball fields. I could see the shock in her facial expression. She continued with the story in detail, describing the kids involved. Her daughter, Laura, is a close friend of Frenchy. She rattled off several other names. "Hold on, Mrs. Booker," I said, as I listened to her open up. "I'm very interested in what goes on around these parts. I'm a board member of the port authority in Fairport Harbor and I'd like to hear the details of what went on here."

Mrs. Booker continued with her story. "These kids live in a small community of diverse-valued homes. Because the kids get along so well, they pride themselves in sharing each others property. It is like a commune. They draw upon each other's skills." She retold a story that her daughter's friend, Frenchy, told her. Frenchy was there to see the whole episode unfold. She said the deputy sheriff added a few details but that only added to her concern. It happened like this.

Today the boys in the group are meeting at the Painesville Township Metro Park. Standing on top of the bank, you need to descend about one hundred feet down. It's a fairly steep drop to get to the shore. The shoreline has some erosion that has stripped away chunks of the bank over the years. The kids around the area know the trails to follow that will take them down the bank to the lake.

The girls in the group had a sleepover and missed the major part of the mission today. They will link up with the boys as the cell phone activity will liven up the late morning risers. Frenchy is on the phone to Laura. He's talking fast and furious, so she hasn't grasped his vernacular. He's been working with her to improve her French. Today he is so excited, he just isn't slowing down. He's talking about a washed-up package they've discovered on the shore. He's mixing his French and English together. "Good grief, Frenchy, we'll be over soon."

As they open the last wrapping, an astonished look comes over the landlubbers. "Gosh, this looks like some big-time fireworks," said Jose. Bones, the head trooper, is the leader of the troop. He directs his brother to run home and let their mom know what's going on. "Tell Mom not to worry. We found a bomb or dynamite floating in the lake. Tell mom I'm taking charge; she better call the police." Willie and Bones, the elders of the troop at fourteen years old, are brothers true. They are like twins, but Bones is a little bit stockier and ten months older. Willie is the fastest runner in the class. "Jason and Blabber, go to the top of the hill and signal when the police come into view. Frenchy will guard our west flank. Frenchy, make sure nobody comes this way," Bones commands. Bones knew this was no ordinary find. Bones has this certain character trait. He's a take-charge person. He was already recognized as the middle school standout. He saw that caution sticker on the side of the plastic bag. This was evidence enough for him that they were dealing with some bad stuff. The pack says the contents are extremely dangerous. Keep cool. Explosive. Bones says to the others, "Hey guys, the person who wrote on the package must know us. Keep cool, explosive. That's us, all right."

The phone rings at the sheriff's station. The dispatcher takes the call in the command center. It is a 911 call from a Painesville Township resident who lives along the lakefront. A mother reports that children have found what appear to be explosives on the lake shore. Their children were playing at the Lake Metro Park.

"One of the children has found a plastic sack containing what would appear to be fireworks or worse." Get right over there Dave, says the dispatcher.

Lake County Sheriff's deputies are sent to the park to investigate. Two squad cars show up within minutes of each other.

Jason, the lookout, was waiting in the parking lot. He realizes that he shouldn't have had that pop. He was losing his battle with nature. Whispering to himself, "I can hold it." He thought about abandoning his post but this assignment was his big chance to gain a stripe with the troop. His friend, Bones, issued urgent orders. I'm to make sure the police are directed to the spot over the bank where the newfound treasure is located. He was so appreciative when he saw the sheriff cruiser's flashing lights. He waves his arms to the patrol cars, pointing to the spot over the bank. As the officers approached, they could tell Jason had an immediate order of business to take care of. "The bomb is over the bank, sir. I have to go pee. I'll be right back, officers," Jason says, as he makes a mad dash to the restroom across the street. As Jason is running for the restroom he yells to the police, "Blabber will show you how to get over the bank without sliding down on your butt." "Come on, sir, this way, hurry. I'm glad you're here, officers. Bones is down there with Jason, Jose, and Frenchy. They have the stuff. It's a good thing we were here officer. That stuff could have hit the rocks and blown up somebody," says Blabber. Blabber continues talking until the deputy says, "Stay back son. Go to the far side of the parking lot. We want all you kids in one safe area."

Soon the officers are descending down the embankment. The way is cobbled together with driftwood steps and pieces of shale rock. It is about a 120-foot descent with the zig and zag to the lake. The officers aren't quite prepared for this trek. Sergeant Dave Gooden and his partner, Rex, finally make it to the site. "What's going on boys?" asks the sergeant. Bones is quick to replay the sequence of events that brought everyone together. "Sir, we were exploring the shore and saw this package floating in the water. We pulled it to shore and opened it. We think this stuff is dangerous."

The officers survey the situation and tell all the boys to abandon their posts. "Thanks boys, we will handle this from here. Leave the immediate area now. The officers on the top of the bank will get your names, says Rex. Sergeant Gooden calls dispatch and requests more help. Deputy Gooden says to the dispatcher, "its dynamite. The kids didn't know for sure but we are securing the area and getting these kids out of here. Send back up, the bomb squad, and notify ATF."

The bomb squad was sent to disable the contents. A search is made of the surrounding area. Metro park rangers aided in the search. The sheriff's patrol boat was used along with the coast guard to make sure more of this material isn't along the shore or in the water. A coast guard patrol boat is sent out to check the area farther from the park. After all departments have secured the area, the ordnance is blown up. The ordinance disposal team decided to blow up the dangerous material right at the metro park rather then risk any further movement.

I told Mrs. Booker that I also am concerned about the security around the lake. I told her to be on guard as a civil defense person. "We need kids and parent that watch for problems. Never take for granted that everybody is friendly around here." I told her.

What Mrs. Booker didn't tell me was the general conversations after the incident.

Later, at the neighborhood playground our youthful detectives were joined by the girls. Frenchy says, "This is a bad sign, guys." They all believe something sinister is going on. They have their own version of what happened. Jason says, "Some fishermen wanted to blow up the waters that hold the walleye. My dad thinks some evil fishermen were making homemade depth charges. That would bring up plenty of fish. He said he remembers finding some nets along the shore a year ago. He says poachers are always trying to build a better trap." Jose seconds the motion that the illegal gill nets were used last year by poachers so they probably decided to try something a little more sophisticated.

Mrs. Booker, who joins the kids at the playground, says, "The whole neighborhood is talking about the dynamite. "We are keeping a close watch on the lake shore. We are the shoreline detectives Mrs. Booker." Jose says. The kids all reaffirm that idea. Mrs. Booker is careful about affirming the detective idea. She says, "Please kids, let the police handle anything like this."

The parents are wondering aloud at the dinner tables that evening. With all the trouble going on in the world nowadays, who wouldn't be a little rattled? Jason's mom asks, "This is such a quiet place. Nobody would bother us, right?"

CHAPTER 23

❀

Inside the Store

The Arab terrorists have set up a number of cover businesses around the Great Lakes Basin over the years. These small food stores and marinas have well-established roots born from legitimate operators of the past. They have a goal—staying connected with the local community. Small food stores offer a business style that can be bought and run without much fanfare. Once in these stores, it is only a matter of serving the community. A good business style is to donate to the local causes. Local folks are permitted to put their posters and business news in the store windows. Some local students are hired to work in the store as stock and checkout clerks.

Safe houses are rented to keep certain cell members hidden. These cell members are the ones who are expendable and have no chance of being able to learn the local language. The stores generate enough cash to keep the cell members that are in hiding supplied with food and shelter. They will wear the suicide belts. Handguns and ammunition are kept hidden in the store office. Explosives, the bombers belts, machine guns, and other special tools of the terrorist are put away in the store safe to be used when the day of infamy is arrives.

A supercell leader and store owner, Abdul Mahdi, is a business man. Mr. Mahdi is also a spiritual leader with a good deal of Western education. He came from Canada two years ago to run this local store. He uses cell middle managers to keep his store running. This frees him to help Captain Awad with planning and coordinating. He is somewhat jealous of Captain Awad's desire to be near Omma. He didn't see the attachment right away but could read this affection in Omma's words regarding Captain Awad. His own lust for Omma causes him to select Omma as one of his middle managers. He worked Omma into the store operation so she could pick up the Western lingo. He has more on his mind than just trying to shape Omma's Western culture.

Omma's private duties included using her past expertise in assembling bombs. Abul Mahdi would make sure Omma was in the store office with him. It is here that Omma realized what Mr. Mahdi had on his mind. She was forced to confront Mr. Mahdi's sexual desires. He was not a gentleman.

"Mr. Mahdi I'm not ready for you," Omma is almost apologetic as Abdul Mahdi pins Omma against the back wall of his office. He's lost control of himself. He holds her arms as she squirms to free herself. His offensive embrace is too much for Omma. She is forced to deliver a counter blow to his manhood. With a right knee she sends him to the floor, her military training circumventing Mr. Mahdi's unwelcome sexual mischief. Omma shucks off Mr. Mahdi's advances with this forgiving advice. "Mr. Mahdi, you have to learn how to handle a Russian woman." Omma says, "I wish Captain Awad wasn't so busy. My heart still has room to share with another man. It is not you, Mr. Mahdi."

Abdul Mahdi painfully says, "Omma, I'm sorry. You are so beautiful. I lost my way."

Many different customers come and go from the store. No one takes notice of the fact that an enemy is building within the area. With a store is a perfect front, a perfect cover.

Inside the store, late-night duties are being carried out to prepare for the final assault. Special chemicals arrive throughout the day disguised as legitimate goods. Care is taken to see that the supercell leader receives the delivery. When the legitimate goods are mixed in the proper order, another use is borne—one that will provide the Mardi Gras with real fireworks. Special delivery trucks arrive and only the boss handles those goods. He keeps these early morning deliveries to a minimum so as not to draw attention. Late-night delivery of weaponry, fuses, remote controls, dynamite, and ammunition all must be kept out from the noses of the lower employees. The delivery is made by a white newspaper van. What appears to be newspaper and magazine deliveries are goods that need to be tucked away for later use. Inside a bundle of magazines, a pistol is hidden. It all takes many deliveries over a year to stock up on all the implements of war.

Each store has its own cache. The stores are mission sensitive. One store will carry equipment for the water-extraction team. Another will be responsible for the upriver mission. A third will work the waterfront Mardi Gras demolition team.

The southern store will keep supplies and house secondary development personnel. It will never open for business, but will always be preparing to open. During the last three weeks, all activity there will make it appear the store is preparing to open. A garage is attached to the south store. A truck and auto, purchased weeks before the operation is put in motion, need to be stored in the garage. During the final weeks before the mission, modifications to the truck are made inside the garage. This will be handy to refurbish the truck bed to handle the mortar placement.

"We shall have a final meeting in the basement of the South store where launch orders are finalized. July 1 is when we meet. Mr. Big, the great one, has said our 11:00 PM final meeting will provide all people one day to rest. During the early morning of July 3, we will load mission-critical equipment. By noon we shall have everything set," says Mr. Mahdi to his middle managers.

Mr. Mahdi needed to keep a few lower employees around to carry out the normal store operations this day. His middle managers aren't always around to help. The routine of the store must still go on. "It is sometimes very troublesome to keep those inquisitive students minding only store operations, especially at closing time," Mr. Mahdi recalls. "Stacey and Tasha are two Mr. Mahdi has to watch. "They may just unknowingly stumble onto the real purpose of the store," Mr. Mahdi says to himself.

He had to leave the store one night. It was one of those situations where he didn't have a middle manager handy. This left the two girls alone to close the store.

Mr. Mahdi keeps the cameras poised at the private room door. There was an incident when those two girls had boyfriends come by to pick them up. They didn't just lock the store and set the manual alarm. This alarm will signal Mr. Mahdi and he knows that they have locked down the store. Mr. Mahdi doesn't use an automatic main alarm at his store. Normally, he sets his own alarm or uses his middle managers to do that.

He didn't receive that customary signal. Remotely, he activated his echo system. This monitors sounds in the private room.

Somehow, Stacey and Tasha entered my private office, which is normally locked, with their boyfriends. The hormones of the two couples must have been in full bloom. Mr. Mahdi listens. He could hear the sounds of zippers and spare change hitting the floor. Mr. Mahdi was many miles away and thought the worst. "They may discover the secrets of the store," he thought. His luck was with him that late night. Zim, his pet parakeet, wasn't use to his uninvited guests. Mr. Mahdi keeps Zim's cage door ajar and he provided a lighter message then the one Mr. Mahdi would have delivered to those girls. He might have been brutal if he got there. Nobody endangers the mission. Zim took care of this affair.

He made his usual no-noise flight. As always, he went to my small desk light and switched it on, giving his customary greeting, "Hello bucko." He sure finished what I couldn't. He handled things far better than I could have hoped. My hidden camera wasn't activated that day. "Damn, I'm sure Zim was treated to an X-rated show." Based on the scramble I could hear, I decided that those invaders won't be prying into my operation anymore. At least when the room says "private," I mean private to Zim and me. I need not tip Stacey and Tasha that I overheard their plight. They may not know how close they were to ending their employment and maybe more. Every now and then I hear Zim say, "You're big." I'm sure he's talking about my height. I found a quarter on the floor of the office the next morning. That was the change I heard hitting the floor last night.

I may have forgotten to lock my private room and the girls wandered in. That is a very big mistake. There is no need to have the lock changed on the office door. Mr. Big would surely kill me if he found out I almost slipped up. The storage locker in the private room has a combination lock on it. The combination lock is still resting on thirty so I know they didn't case out the room. My other safe places are in order. The store secrets are still safe.

CHAPTER 24

Something Is Brewing

Mary Ann was contemplating her next move. She was concerned—even worried—that her river business was somehow being squeezed by new competition upriver. Business is still good. The last week of June is always very busy on the Grand River. These newcomers are outsiders. "They built a boat launch that is going to compete with our business," she tells her brother, John.

Construction crews have been working the land on Fairport's side of the river. They are causing quite a buzz. They've been building at the old Diamond Shamrock property for about three months now. "Grooming the land," is what the mayor says. He always downplays the significance of the work. The speculation is that a sports complex and a golf course are being built. "So what is it?" ask the local folk. Mayor Reese works the question with political diplomacy. He says remedial work needs to be done to improve the environmental impact the old factories had on the land. The secrecy of the whole plan is contained. This is not sitting well with some folks in the area. Mary Ann is one who is asking questions. The workers at the construction site are staying in a couple of trailers. These workers have been secluded, in a sense. Mexican hired helpers are working on that wide open space. "Why can't they leave the property?" Mary Ann asks. She says, "A golf course is in the plans. I think that part of the plan is true. What is going on where the big tent is located?"

The large circus tent that is being used up the river at the construction site has attracted the attention of the locals. A small garrison of private security guards is stationed around this tent area. One of the boaters told her a boat landing has been built there. Mary Ann already knew about that. She will have more competition. This additional business pressure from outsiders is bad for her business. Now the Grand River has a muddy-water streak running out of it where the trailer camp is located. Kids say they are a bunch of cultists or witches always sitting on blankets and bowing to the sun.

Mary Ann finally decides she needs to call somebody with investigative talent. She has two customers who work for the FBI. "I'm calling them," she says to her brother. With that, she places a call to the Cleveland FBI. She reports her story to a call screener. "I've seen shady characters around this area. People are moving things from boats across the river. It just looks suspicious," she tells the call screener. Her commanding nature is present in her voice. She adds a final comment. "You tell Agent Roman, Mary Ann Rutherford called from her boat ramp in Grand River." The call screener was polite and put the call on the back burner. He advises Mrs. Rutherford, "Madam, this matter is a local concern, and you need to contact local authorities." Mary Ann doesn't like the fact that she can't talk to Agent Ron Roman. She says, "That call screener is working off the backs of us taxpayers. He's passing the buck."

A couple days later, by coincidence, Agent Roman calls Mary Ann. "This is Ron Roman, Mrs. Rutherford. How are you?" Agent Roman quickly adds, "Bill Wright and I are coming down to launch my boat at your launch in a few days." Seated nearby, is Agent Wright, who looks up from his desk. "Well that's just fine," says Mary Ann. Mary Ann is convinced her call to the FBI was effective. "I knew you'd get my message, Agent Roman. We have trouble over here. You better come as soon as you can," she says. Agent Roman is caught off guard. "Oh, what's going on?" he asks. Mary Ann tells Agent Roman about the camp upriver and the suspicious activity across from her boat launch. "I heard them speaking Persian or some foreign dialect when they were unloading equipment off their boat the other day. My hearing is something special. I tune into this river. The water will carry sound an incredible distance. Something is fishy around here, and I don't mean walleye," she says. Agent Roman takes in the odd exchange in conversation. He remembers the width of the river and finds Mary Ann's ability to hear sounds across the river as being quite a stretch of one's ability to hear. However, he couples this conversation with what Mr. Stern had to say.

Agent Roman feels he needs to at least do a cursory inspection. The fact that he had a visit from Richard Stern gives a little credence to checking out what's going on.

"Mary Ann, you have those walleye waiting for us, and we'll have a look around." Mary Ann was quite pleased with her actions. She's convinced her call to the FBI got results. "Those FBI people know where their money is coming from," she exclaims.

The two FBI agents discuss their upcoming fishing trip to Grand River.

"We better do a little checking just to be on the safe side while we are over there," says Agent Roman to Agent Wright. Agent Wright says, "We have a big meeting coming up in July with local security forces. The security meeting had been planned for the first week of July where all the local safety forces, police, and high level officials can compare notes about Homeland Security. Because of the holidays it's been decided to wait until the second week in July to meet. Many staff members are out of town and won't be back until then."

Agent Roman says, "It won't hurt to let them know we were in their area. We don't have to tell them we were walleye fishing." They smile at each other knowing that this is more about pleasure than business. They felt pretty good about their plans until their boss came in with important news.

There was a lot more official business going on around Fairport Harbor than the two agents had known about. Their boss gives them a new assignment. The two agents would become part of a greater Cleveland investigative team. "Boss, we have a fishing trip planned for Fairport Harbor," said Agent Roman. "That's fine. I'm sending you two on a big fishing trip. The National Security Agency has been involved in a sweep of the Lake Erie area right where you agents are going. Listen to what I've been told." With that their boss went into details about a broad mission.

"About a month ago Homeland Security became aware of a large volume of boat traffic traveling from Canada and to Canada. Point to point satellite references from Canada across Lake Erie to Lake County and Cuyahoga County threw up a watch flag. Each month satellite data painted a picture of boat tracks and detailed this information for review. The satellite information was relayed to the National Security Agency. A continuous satellite tracking arrangement was ordered for the Lake Erie area based on the monthly review. Border security measures were being improved and this tracking was one of the improvements made to the system. NSA was concerned because of the Buffalo, New York, terrorist cell that was busted by us not long ago. They felt some cell fragments may still remain. The terrorists in this cell came from Canada via Niagara Falls. No one is ready to say the border is clear of problems because the Buffalo cell was taken out. Boat tracks to Fairport Harbor from Canada and back again have been identified. While this wasn't any indication of a problem, NSA decided to do more homework." Their boss continued to tell them the greater picture.

"An undercover agent was assigned to follow up on what is going on around Lake and Cuyahoga Counties in Ohio. National Security Agency decided to use a mole to inspect the property in Fairport Harbor where construction is ongoing. Agent Jane was selected. She arrived at the site driving a dump truck. Her job was to do a closer inspection of the site without creating suspicion. Agent Jane was able to talk to some of the workers at the site when she applied for hauling business as an independent trucker. She told the foreman her truck was idle now and could use some hauling business. Jane is blond, a nice looker, and the foreman quickly sent her over to the main construction trailer. She was hired to haul fill dirt for the golf course. Soon she was making regular trips that kept her bouncing around the site. She made mental notes of the people who seemed to be in charge."

"The developer, Barrie the Lion Builders, was doing site preparation work. People make references to Lord Barrie, who is the owner. She hasn't seen him."

Their boss tells them, "You two will find out more. We see a big tent erected on the property and supposedly it is a place where they are conducting advanced soil testing. Supposedly, chromate contamination is being contained by the tent. We are not so sure of that. Here's what else we know, and how we found out. Security personnel are of two groups. One group provides protection of equipment and hovers around the big tent. The other security detail is mostly low-rank agency types. They watch over perimeter fencing and keep a check on the gates around the site. Agent Jane asked for an additional sleeper to see what was inside of the big tent. This covert operation was handled by Agent Williams. Tex Williams was a star athlete from Graceland College in Iowa. He was a decathlon champ. The reason I bring this up is because you gentlemen may have to work with him. Mr. Roman and Tex should hit it off well together. You two guys probably hit the same bars in Iowa. Tex is well-traveled and saw action in Afghanistan and Iraq. He is a black Texan with a good handle on the Arabic language. His mission was to infiltrate the camp late at night and place a couple of audio sensors by or inside the big tent. He tried to get a photo of the inside of the tent."

Agent Roman and Agent Wright listened intently realizing that a major covert act was going on here.

Their boss continued, "The night Mr. Williams choose was cloudy. If there was a moon out there, it couldn't be seen. The perimeter guards were low-grade security, so it was easy for him to slip in. He cautiously moved about the camp and placed listening devices on the rear of the tent. He managed to take a couple pictures of the inside of the tent. They turned out to be of little value.

Another tent was inside the big tent. The audio plant that was monitoring the tent would prove to be better. The sound of digging was being done each night. It was as if graves were being dug. Someone said they were only two hundred feet down and water was filling the opening and that Mr. Big would have to make a decision on abandoning this project. What we do know from all of this is nothing. They could very well be doing just what they say. You two will check out the reasons for the security. Why all the trips to Canada? Gentlemen, get your fishing gear."

CHAPTER 25

Mr. Big Will Sting

Osama Bin Laden and his gang are getting further squeezed. He was run out of Afghanistan and pushed into the border area of Pakistan and Afghanistan. He is becoming isolated as the noose of justice closes in. No government forces from Pakistan or Afghanistan can say they know where this terrorist icon is located. These governments are searching for him with the added help of the CIA. Pakistani troops are moving into an area where there is opposition. One of Bin Laden's camps near his base was attacked by Pakistani troops with CIA assistance. A Bin Laden security man detailed the battle going on at another camp not far away. They were in a precarious position.

The Taliban fighter's plight was difficult. They were working with Osama Bin Laden. First, they were ambushed by Afghan and American soldiers who drove them to the Pakistani side of the border. They were under attack by helicopter gun ships and small arms fire. Taliban commanders sent word to the Bin Laden camp that they had been mauled. Their retreat was made in haste. They suffered high losses. The battlefield casualties were left to die. This late May onslaught was a terrible time to be driven from what was a secure base. They sent word to their leading commander that the time for retreat from Afghanistan has come.

One of Bin Laden's tribal leaders reported that the American CIA participated in the raid that destroyed his security base near the Taliban camp. Sensing the worst, Bin Laden's group moved their operation. They were able to slip away, but the supreme commander, Osama Bin Laden, was on the run. Yet, he was safe from being captured because of the loyal tribes who shield his whereabouts.

A Bin Laden spy cell in Washington DC received news that a Bin Laden camp was destroyed. Bin Laden was not among those killed. The spy cell soon realized this.

Bin Laden assembled his elders for consultation. Their meeting concluded with a directive to the Washington DC spy cell. "I sent a messenger to Washington to relay a personal message. The heroes are to start the invasion that Mr. Big has been preparing. We cannot wait any longer. Our situation is threatened. We need the American invasion to move ahead."

Clearly Bin Laden was mixed up, confused. His Iraqi commander is gone. His own situation was becoming threatened. He needs Mr. Big's help.

Mr. Big received the order from Bin Laden through the Washington spy cell. Mr. Big would not receive the X bomb. "Iran was not ready to help with that step," said the Washington spy.

At the tent camp, Mr. Big was informed that the well to the salt mine was filling with water. Mr. Big decided to cease construction of the hole to the salt mine. Mr. Big told his lieutenants, "We have not made enough progress at the camp and other factors are involved now." Mr. Big tried to hide his disappointment. He would think of an alternative plan.

"Since the X bomb hasn't been delivered, we now need to act on the big picture," says an agitated Mr. Big. "We will modify the attack. The whole construction group will be sent back to Canadian bases.

Mr. Big doesn't waste any time. He has his lieutenants rent a small armada of ferry boats from a boat livery nearby. The next day after modifying the ferries, he orders his lieutenants to have all men, women, and children evacuate to the nearby marina. They will board the awaiting boats and sail north. Everyone not associated with the final mission is to be ferried back to the Canadian marina. The three large party boats are loaded with passengers for the trip back. Everyone was told of the impending holiday. A break in the toil of construction is needed. Planes in Canada will shuttle anyone wanting to vacation elsewhere.

As the last group boarded the boats a curious onlooker was keeping tabs on the group. Mary Ann watched the three new craft arrive. These party boats are taking the foreigners out of here in mass. They didn't appear to be going fishing. Luggage and heavy equipment was loaded on to the boats. Soon an escort yacht was leading this flotilla out of the harbor. Maybe it is an exercise in boater safety. The thirty-six foot yacht was like a shepherd watching the sheep. The party boats aligned themselves and followed the leader yacht. All the passengers were decked out in red life preservers which must have pleased the coast guard as they passed the station. They past the harbor entrance sailing by the lighthouse. The boats started to head northwest as if going to the fishing hot spot. They were well out into the lake and on a single pipe of the boatswains mates whistle the boats turn. The heading is due north. The wind was blowing to the northeast. If they kept their course they should land near the Canadian marina.

After about two hours, the boats were far out now. Land was no where to be seen. The thirty-sixer increased speed and moved well ahead of the pack. The other boats did likewise, struggling to keep up. The captain of each boat started to let the children steer the boats but took command as they needed to catch up to the thirty-sixer. A fun time was being had on a relaxing voyage. The wind was aiding their getaway trip. They must have been about 30 miles out in the middle of the lake. Mr. Big, the captain of the thirty-sixer picked up his cell phone and made a call. Suddenly, without warning the life preservers on everyone on the party boats started to erupt in a great explosion. The party boats exploded from underneath the waterline. The scene was quickly littered with debris, human remains, and a cloud of smoke. So quick was the explosion and fire that the lake seemed to blink an eye and erase much of the carnage. The wind blew the smoke from the scene. What was once a heavenly voyage turned into a watery grave site. Missing was the tombstones. Only the seagulls seemed to be ready to pick apart the minuscule pieces of a boat ride to hell.

The thirty-sixer made a couple of passes over the trail of death to make sure all were lost. The wind will scattered the pieces. Mr. Big was pleased that this execution was done so well. He made sure the evidence was scattered by plowing through the area at high speed. His wake would push apart anything clinging to some last gasp effort to stay afloat. He continued his journey to the north for about five miles and doubled back to Fairport Harbor. This way he could pass by once more to prove to himself that the job was done right. Soon the big plan will be started.

The idea that they could alter the course of the river was proven by the Diamond Alkali Company years ago. That company did change the river's path many years ago. Mr. Big's plan was to drain the river into the salt company's mine. His window of opportunity was closing as Independence Day was only six days away. He needed another year beyond the six days of digging that was left. If he set a massive charge into the existing dig he might be able to buckle the mine below by virtue of a man-made shock. The accompanying earthquake would cause a tidal wave in Lake Erie that would disrupt the entire Great Lakes ecosystem. His diabolical mind refused to let the plan die. "I will rewrite history as the great one who brought America to its knees."

Mr. Big had a chemical engineering degree from the College De France in Paris. That was a distant memory for him. He was fifty-two years old. Constantly fighting and devoting his time to the Islamic cause was his way of life. Now he needed to conjure up a revision to a plan that lacked the X bomb. Without the X bomb, his ultimate device for activating an earthquake, the plan is doomed. Mr. Big's emotions switch from delight to despair.

He knows deep down that his great dig is far off the mark. He needed much greater depth. The amount of pyrotechnic he has is not enough to ensure a great collapse of the mine. The special X device did not come as he expected. He is deviating from the master plan. Somewhat crazed, he does an emotional flip. His faith would make it happen.

"My sapper cell will enter the salt mine and set charges on weight-bearing columns near our excavation. A catastrophic failure in the mine may still work if I have luck on my side." Mr. Big started to think out loud. "This plan would move to flank speed. Send out orders to the stores to remove some of their fuel from the gas pumps. "We will fill the shaft with gasoline and chemical mix. We have stored a quantity of fertilizer and fuel oil which can also be mixed together." Mr. Big became inflamed, enraged. He was a perfectionist. He did not like the fact that he was deviating from his original, well-thought-out plan. He issued orders to his lieutenants. "Base primer charges will be set at the bottom of the shaft. The explosive will rupture the earth. An ensuing earthquake made by my hands will open the salt mine. The Grand River will empty into the massive hole. The sting borne by this operation will be a testimony from Al-Qaeda. Our statement will be complete and the world will know that America has been invaded. I shall rule as the terror takes hold of Middle America. People all over the world will hail to our principles. I will send orders in two days to prepare for the final mission. Sting, sting, will happen." Coded messages are relayed to store cells. Internet codes tell store cells the final meeting is upon us. Stores in Fairport Harbor, Painesville, Painesville Township are the ones who become activated. Internet codes hide the elaborate scheme. Supercell leaders are now thrust into action in preparing the stores for participation. The stores must move their equipment into vans for transport to the yachts they are assigned to outfit. Guns and ammunition will be moved to forward positions with the team of sappers.

The safe house that housed the brothers Abdulah and Ahmed along with Islam Sahebah and El Hahurdi are visited by Captain Awad. "I'm here to let you know we are close to the beginning of battle. I will take you men to the proper stores when the time comes." Saheed Abdulah and his brother, Ahmed, have been tucked away waiting for their chance to become martyrs. Explosive belts will be issued to the two suicide heroes a few hours before the fireworks go on display. The forward store, Fairport Harbor, will supply the belts. Islam Sahebah and El Hahurdi, the sappers, will work with Mr. Big and his crew on the *thirty-sixer*.

Canadian marina yachts will launch on demolition day. Captain Awad has concluded that they may need more boats for the mission. "Crews of hardened soldiers will commandeer and man stolen yachts. Boat owners and operators may be summarily shot and thrown overboard," says the captain.

The ruthless portion of the mission will have no prisoners. Anyone in the way will become a victim of the terror plot.

Commandeered boats will be used to back up the main flotilla if needed. The two smaller yachts, the thirties, will arrive at the loading area across from our unloading zone upriver. They will be fitted with necessary armament to carry out their assignment. The shuttle boat will pick up Mr. Big at the circus tent boat launch and take him to the *thirty-sixer*. Mr. Big will board the *thirty-sixer* and head up the river to drop off the sappers, Islam Sadebah and El Hahurdi at the mine. These two sappers have also been salted away so as not to draw attention to themselves. The *thirty-sixer* will wait at the drop-off zone to pick up the salt company sappers. Then it is time to take down the coast guard station and head out to watch our fireworks.

The Soviet women will leave the Painesville Township cell store and take up a holding position at the Eagles Nest restaurant. They will receive a cell phone message to ignite the forest and nearby community. They shall not be challenged. If they must protect the mission, they are to eliminate any intruders.

All parties will synchronize the operation by listening to the AM radio station WTPM, 1000 on the radio dial. At the 6:00 PM news hour, you will set watches. You will receive an advertisement via radio message for (*sting*) the bee sting medicine or an abort mission cell phone call. Should the mission face an abort mission, (*dive*) will be seen on the cell phone display. All equipment shall be thrown overboard on your way back to the Canadian marina. You will be helped by cell phone calls if you need assistance. You may be on your own if you receive an abort-mission call. Anchored out on the lake will be the freighter *Gupka*. It will be there ready to set sail and take all members to Buffalo, New York. An exit from Dock #5 will be done by auto. Be at the used car dealership of Lemmon Tree on July 5, at 10:00 AM. Mullah Omar will meet you. Your next stop will be messaged on the glove box cell phone.

Mr. Big has planted special phones among his subordinates that are used to either move the mission ahead or terminate a member by his command. He has no problem eliminating anyone who is failing.

By day minus three all planning was complete. Each cell member was assigned a task by the supercell leaders. Each store supercell leader monitored the Internet Arabica site. The newspapers also coded the same messages. These paid advertisements kept all local cells and super leaders aware of each member's status. The radio station was paid for a short advertisement. "Go, Go. Now you know." It will air just before the 6:00 PM news. Any snafus at this point would present dire straits for success.

Al Jazeera was used as the world paper to report the progress of supercell operations. World communications via the newspaper is preferred because the CIA was monitoring Internet communications. The freighter *Gupka* would need to be in position so it was told of progress by the marina base in Canada. Time was nearing to Sting.

Minus day two is upon us. We are now hunkered down, resting.

CHAPTER 26

❈

It Is Going to Sting

Richard got up early to work on a photo album of a girls softball team. The photos he took are excellent which is quite remarkable since he's been binge drinking. He won't have to doctor these photos. He spent about four hours assembling his work. "Now it's time for a cold one," he says as he looks to the studio clock. His mind is still clouded from a late night out at the bar. He hasn't slept much in the last few days, preferring to put a buzz on. "Is 11:00 AM to early to socialize? No, I need a little head start" says Richard to the only objects around, his photos. He hears the traffic outside his home. Mardi Gras visitors are starting to come into town. It's fireworks night. The beach will be one big party. Party people will be exploding firework at all times. The entire festival is full of bangs and booms each day.

Richard's days run together as he keeps a steady diet of booze running in his veins. He's running on empty but the party atmosphere goes on.

He twists off a beer cap and takes a dose. Richard acts as if he is administering a sedative to himself. "Ahhh, my work's done and it is party time. I might have to stop at the clubs today. His foreign war service allows him to be a member of the local VFW. His Hungarian heritage allows him to be a member of another club. He has abused the social value of the clubs over the years, choosing to cultivate his growing alcohol dependence.

With the thought of the clubs in his head, he does just that. He visits both clubs and spends a fair amount of time in each. After consuming six or so beers and a couple shots of blackberry brandy, he heads home. He orders a pizza and has another beer at home. As he waits for the pizza delivery person, he falls asleep.

Just that quick he started to dream.

The yachts are traveling south from the Canadian marina. It is a sailor's dream day as the waters are blown by a mild wind from the south. The two-foot waves are not slowing the travel. On board the boats are men of evil. The terrorists, with faces looking into the breeze, are masking the reasons for this boat trip. I see the hateful, vengeful men heading to an epiphany. The mood on the chugging watercraft is a controlled wretchedness. These men are ready to do harm to America.

They will be crossing the border and entering American waters. The two smaller yachts slow down and separate from the bigger yacht. They decide to separate. They wish to be viewed as fishermen, not as a big armada. The big yacht starts moving pretty fast. Alas, they have arrived. The miniature Trojan horse is here. It comes into Fairport's harbor about 5:30 PM.

I have to call Mayor Reese and sound the warning.

They are watching the Mardi Gras partygoers lining the waterfront. Festivities are in full swing. They start down the Grand River. The targets are ripe to be picked apart. The thirty-sixer passes the coast guard station and the salt mine. The thirty-sixer has slowed down as it heads down the river. The sleepy pace of travel conceals the thunder and lightning about to be unleashed by the men on this craft. Right now they can't afford to become a suspicious craft.

The doorbell rings and Richard is thankfully brought out of a nightmare. He stumbles over to the door. It's the pizza delivery guy. Richard pays the young man with a five and a ten. "Keep the change," says the disheveled Richard. "Thanks for the tip, sir." The young pizza delivery man says.

He steadies his late lunch on the kitchen counter. Richard struggles to open the box and starts to wrestle with the first slice. This is just what he needs. He has one slice and decides he better not get too full. He wants to see the fireworks.

His little nightmare passes him by. It didn't stick, in his sloshed up state. What he needs is one more beer to think about that dream and then a shower. He's got over a half dozen beers remaining in the party pack. He pops another tab and tries to remember the dream. He downs two more beers and says, "I need a shot of vodka. That'll jog my memory." Richard knocks over his beer but manages to get the cabinet door open. He pulls out the quart bottle. It has two-thirds remaining. Richard doesn't take a chance pouring a shot. He lifts the bottle to his lips. He half gulps the spirits. He quickly grabs the fallen beer can and uses the remaining beer to wash down the Russian vintage. He looks at the label on the vodka bottle. This seems to help him connect to the dream. "Fine Russian Spirits," he says. "That's it. The Russians are coming." He carries the bottle of vodka to his bedroom. The clock on the nightstand says 6:25 PM. He takes another drink as he tries to assemble what this dream is about. He takes another drink. "The Russians are coming," he says as his head hits the headboard.

In the meantime, out in the waters of Grand River, what is really happening?

The men of this terrorist mission are becoming tense. The face of the helmsman has the look of a hockey player before the big game. Will they be stopped? The terrorists are passing the coast guard station and any inspection of their craft will likely turn into a shootout. The *thirty-sixer* continues down the river, stopping at the marina before the tent city boat ramp. This is the exchange zone. One crew member changes boats and uses a small craft to travel farther up the river to the construction site boat launch. Here, Mr. Big comes aboard. He is waiting as if he is the bait on a hook ready to feed the unsuspecting towns. He has his briefcase which is loaded with cash and cell phones. He takes the helm and steers the boat back up the river. They board the *thirty-sixer* again. This operation is making a final approach. This is the point of no return. He grips the boat's wheel, white-knuckled hands feeling for the sensitivity of the rudder cables that turn the boats motor. The mood is spontaneous, deliberate, and serious. Mr. Big is standing erect, about to enter World War III.

Omma has parked the truck at the Eagles Nest's parking lot. She and the other two women, Hilmah and Camallah, pray that they will succeed. "Ladies," says Omma, "we are going forward with Captain Awad's plan. Load your handguns, load the AKs." Hilmah, riding in the back bench seat, uncovers the weapons they brought from the Painesville Township store. A crate holds plenty of ammunition as she forces clips into the machine guns.

Omma is teary-eyed as she thinks of Captain Awad. Camallah, sensing the emotional drain of this mission, grabs the hand of Omma. "Omma, you are the strong one," she says. "Camallah, I must share with you a secret in my heart. I love Captain Awad," Omma confesses to her trusted soldier friends. "I stay focused," says Omma as she fights off her emotional dip.

Omma punches on the gas pedal of the truck. They head down Olive Street in Grand River village and abruptly stop. She turns onto Route 44 heading north. Hilmah looks over the gear stowed in the back of the truck bed. The mortar mount is sticking up but covered by a blanket. The shells are stored next to the mount. Omma skillfully maneuvers the truck into the parking lot where they will start the attack. They quickly disembark near the Mentor Marsh. They are hidden from the road by a hedge row of bushes and young trees. They set up the mortar launch on the opposite side of the truck, which will further shield the launcher from the road. They have set up their attack according to the supercell leader's instructions. The mortar rounds are laid out in rows according to the charge they will use. Magnesium charged explosives are laid out with a few smoke charges. The smoke charges should confuse and disorient everyone responding. They have white smoke, black smoke and red smoke charges. Captain Awad said, "Use the red smoke charge last. The leaders will know your attack is finished. This charge is designed to give off a large plume into the sky."

The women expertly deploy the equipment in short order. The engagements with each other have turned squarely Russian. They have dropped the fake American identity. Omma, pointing in the direction, says in Russian, "*Priama, priama*." They have mentally rehearsed this part of the mission over and over.

With the motor running in the truck and the radio tuned to WTPM, the signal comes in.

"This is a commercial message from Sting, the good-bye itch cream. It's time for your medicine, now buy Sting. Those pesky bugs will be compelled to sting soon. Buy the super formulation that relieves the bite from those bugs that invade this part of the country."

"That is the message, the signal, the plan is birthing. Final orders will be coming soon," says Omma. The women must wait and be prepared to eliminate anyone that comes close to their fire base. They have experienced this moment in the past. The taste of war has soured their mind. Other battles they have fought in give them some comfort. Hilmah realizes she is the invader. She needs to be calm. Still, the moment is quite exhilarating.

Hilmah has an AK machine gun ready to fire. Any passing car could pull into this lonely parking lot. The area is a nature preserve but never receives much traffic.

Mr. Big hears the radio message about STING. He picks up his cell phone and makes connection with Omma. "You need to sting. Omma copy, Omma fire. Omma fire." Mr. Big has given the command. Much is riding on their fate. The women must set up the diversion. At this point Mr. Big is watching and listening for the explosions that will mean the women have started their attack.

The time is about 6:40 PM. Seconds tick away, he waits. Time is now an eternity.

Omma's cell phone beeps. She answers the call. Her hand is above her head. Now nodding her head up and down, she lowers her arm. "Fire!" Her voice is passionate. She signals, and waves with her hand. "Copy! Great One," says Omma.

Immediately, Camallah releases the load into the mortar tube. Thump, whosh; thump, whoosh; thump, whooshing sound of the rounds as they are fired. The first three go into the forest of dead wood and decaying trees. The women adjust the mortar placement for a new target. Thump, whoosh; thump, whoosh; thump, whoosh goes three more times. The mortar rounds are fired. Kaboom, boom, boom. A few more seconds tick away. Kaboom, boom, boom. This time shells are sent into the community of houses. They load the smoke rounds. Thump, whoosh; thump, whoosh; thump goes the red marker smoke round. Whoosh, it's airborne.

The air now starts to take on the smell of burning wood. Those mortar round explosions are deafening. The calm neighborhood is on fire. The calm quickly turns to anguish, distress, and mayhem.

A man is running in the street with clothes on fire. He still has a paintbrush in his hand as shock takes over his body. His house was decapitated by the second explosion. The first round sent shards of concrete into houses. Windows are blown out ten houses from the impact area. The incendiary charges have created numerous fires. The confusion is rampant. Residents don't know if they should stay in their houses or evacuate the area. Some cars are pulling out of drives and lining the road. Those drivers have made a conscious decision to get the hell out.

Siren, start to wail. This is the next signal Captain Awad told the women to listen for. It is the signal to leave the area before the next reaction takes hold. Quickly, the women throw the equipment into the back of the truck. They take off heading back along the river. They can hear sirens blare out the notes of distress. They pullover to let the oncoming police pass.

It takes the women five minutes to get to the communications tower. Omma grabs the satchel of charges. She instructs the two other women to start cutting the fence surrounding the tower. Omma guards the two as they work through the links. They cut a woman-size hole in the fence and crawl inside. Omma passes the satchel to Camallah. She pulls the charges from the satchel and presses them to the tower. Hilmah tapes over the charges, two on one side. They drop the satchel seven feet from the tower. She sets a motion detector to explode in the satchel if it is moved. The red blinking light indicates it will arm in sixty seconds. In seven minutes they have the whole job done and ready. Omma says, "Let's go!" They climb through the fence and are on the road again. Omma is driving the truck.

By using cell phone control they can drive away and blow up the tower. Camallah dials the activator phone number. "Omma, are you ready?" Camallah asks. "*Niet!*" No, she says in Russian. Omma drives the truck to the top of the entrance ramp where they can get a clear view of the tower. "Now!" *Boom*, off goes the charges. The tower starts to lean over like a crooked old man. As it starts to fall, the motion switch sets off the satchel charge which blows the tower from its base. The tower lands across the road that separates the two villages. Cars are blocked by the fallen tower.

The women have completed the first part of their mission. Omma picks up speed and then slows down to cut across the divided highway. She is now going east on Ohio Route 2. Their next stop will be the nuclear plant. So far all is right on schedule with the women. The women give high fives to each other. Their faces shine with happiness as they know Captain Awad will be pleased. The precision of the attack is very professional. The women think to themselves in private that they are doing the work of their religion. Camallah is not entirely gleeful as she has reservations about attacking civilians.

Mr. Big is proud and happy. Having heard the first blast, he knows the women have mastered the first episode of the mission. Two more explosions go off. He slowly plows ahead. Another *boom, boom, boom* continues. "Now we play with their lives," he says to one of his lieutenants.

Mr. Big pulls up to the rocky shore where he drops off the two sappers by the salt mine shaft. Security is no match for these two. They make the two security guards open the shaft elevator. The lightning speed of a knife attack and the elevator doorman is silenced. They have the guards lead the way into the salt mine. Each man has three detonators with timers and three satchels weighing forty-five pounds. It is all dynamite. They set the charges on the columns that they figure will cause a buckling of the earth. Timers are set for forty-five minutes. They are fast in working with this deadly equipment. Away they go. They have more messy chores to take care of. Without any expression, they turn to their commandeered security guards. The sappers carry silencer pistols and use them to blank any comments from the guards.

Back to the route that brought them down the shaft. They enjoy the ride up. Once up and out, they take off their backpacks and hand carry only the pistols.

They run full speed to get to the awaiting boat. They flip the pistols to the lieutenants guarding Mr. Big.

Mr. Big is composed as another piece of action is working like a fine Swiss watch. There is a cloud of smoke funneling up to the south of them. The women have hit the second target. The communications tower is out of order. The *thirty-sixer* starts to move on. It's time to head north, out into the lake. "First we will load our rocket-propelled grenade launchers for the dismantling of the coast guard station," says Mr. Big. They don't make any secret of their intentions now.

As the *thirty-sixer* nears the station the men take aim at the barracks and office. The coast guard rescue boat is hit next and it flips the boat on its side as if harpooned. The scene is almost movie-like as people standing on the pier watch in horror as the blaze of fire is taking down the coast guard station. Everyone is frantic and frightened.

Using a two-way radio, Mr. Big calls the two yachts. They are near Fairport's beach. "You may sting," says Mr. Big. "All is going so well we need to start the shelling now." It is 8:30 PM. The mine explosives go off in a thunder that shakes the floor of the salt mine. This is followed by systematic thumps of mortars being fired from the two yachts. One, two, three, four, trajectory shots are fired into the Mardi Gras midway. The beach scene has bathers running from the water and others running into the water. Pandemonium sets in. The Mardi Gras trailers are blowing up from the mortar attack. Before Mr. Big's eyes is colossal destruction. Fair rides are blown apart. The Ferris wheel rolls off its axis. People are dangling from the ride like linen on a clothes line.

The two yachts off the coast of Fairport Harbor are scoring some more points with salvo after salvo going boom, boom. Each blast leaves men, women, and child running for their lives. Victims are littering the Mardi Gras grounds. More of the same is happening again and again as explosive charges rip apart food stands. Smoke is billowing over the entire midway. Sirens are wailing as tent fires are blazing all over the place. People are staggering, running, and walking like Halloween zombies. The deafening booms go off without a noticeable break in the action.

The sappers wearing the bombers belts waste no time in running up to the sheriff's trailer. Kaboom, as the suicide belt, which seems to be made in hell, blows the trailer off its foundation. The fireball consumes nearby tents as people are reduced to blackened char around the fragments of the suicide bombers. A mad dash of grief-stricken Mardi Gras patrons moves up High Street to get out of harm's way. Suddenly, another rat-a-tat-tat goes off from the snipers machine guns hidden in the lighthouse tower. The terrorists mow down citizens indiscriminately. The street is littered with wounded bodies and corpses. This is hell in high fever. The men in the tower quickly throw several bottles of gasoline to the ground. There machine gun blasts ignite the fuel. A serpentine rolling fire curls down the intersections of High Street and Second Street. Down the hill the fuel fire travels.

Omma and her crew arrive near the site of the power plant. All is not well here. A patrol car is stopped by the south gate. They can't set up to fire as planned. They continue down the road looking for another target to attack. They have been mission perfect so far.

Omma says, "We will go back to our original plan." The women discuss how to take out the security car where they first intended to strike.

"We don't want to draw attention," says Camallah. "I'll knock him off. Drop me off by his car and I'll pretend you two told me to walk home."

"I'll tell him I befriended you," says Hilmah. Omma takes charge and says, "Grab your pistols and finish him. No more of this planning. Just act like you are lost and pop him." Omma isn't one for dramatics.

Hilmah and Camallah grab their silent pistols. They pull up to the parked security guard and roll down their window. "Sir, we are lost. Where is Townline Road?" The guard isn't too concerned about the pretty good looking girls but his security radio is abuzz with news about problems in Grand River. He doesn't have time to react. Thud, thud, thud, as the two women begin firing from the truck door window. Point-blank range is doom to the guard. He slumps down inside the car.

Hilmah jumps to the back of the truck and sets up the mortar. Camallah loads the mortar for successive shots into the power plant. They fire three times but can't get a good feel for the intended target. Omma watches as the mortar charges fall way off target. Omma says, "Damn, Hilmah, you are going back to mortar school. That's enough, abandon the mortar."

Hilmah throws the mortar placement into the bushes. They jump back into the cab. Away Omma goes. She's speeding down the road as this part of the mission is not going well. Omma calls Mr. Big for instructions. "Oh, Great One, we have failed the power plant operation. We are making our escape now. What shall we do?" "Omma, asks Mr. Big. Mr. Big responds. "Open the glove box and press 3-2-1-1-1-1-1 on the red cell phone. You will receive new instructions on how to abandon your truck and where you will go next."

"Yes, sir," says Omma. She tells Camallah to grab the red cell phone out of the glove box. Omma speeds down the road. "You dial. 3-2-1-1-1-1-1," demands Omma. Omma is a little perturbed by the way things just went.

Camallah dials 3-2-1-1-1 and stops. Do we need to dial 1 and then 4-4-0 or 2-1-6," asks Camallah.

"I don't know. He didn't say. Just dial 3-2-1-1-1-1-1," Omma says. Camallah punches in 3-2-1 and then Omma says, "Cops." Camallah stops the dial. The two passengers grab their weapons.

Camallah grabs a hand grenade from under her seat and hands it to Hilmah. Camallah says. "Use this. Throw it under his car as you plug him. Jump into the bed of the truck as we drive away."

Omma slows down and pulls over to the side of the road. "Take him out," Omma says. The officer pulls behind the truck. Hilmah jumps from the passenger side of the truck and fires into the driver's side windshield. She pulls a pin on a hand grenade and rolls it under the police car.

"Go," Hilmah says, as she jumps into the back of the pickup. The hand grenade blows the police car off the side of the road. Camallah sets down her pistol and picks up the red cell phone. She dials 3-2-1-1-1-1-1. Boom, the truck does a backflip and is engulfed in flames. Hilmah is launched like the mortar shell they just fired. She hits the asphalt road in a thud. They are gone.

The sappers in the lighthouse tower decide it is time to pack up and join the others at the pickup zone. They descend the tower. A mad dash is made going down the steep, grassy bank north of the lighthouse. The trio fast step to the parking lot where boat trailers and cars are parked among one another. It is 9:30 PM.

The *thirty-sixer* comes swooping in and retrieves the terrorists. The boat roars off heading northeast with its lights off. The silhouette of fire is dancing along the shoreline. The cry of help and the call of siren slowly fade away. Soon all the working cell boats are out of the harbor. Escaping by boat is in the plans, and this whole *nightmare of a night* is playing out like a horror movie. The pack of terrorists are all working their way north in the darkness, using a global-positioning device as their director. The two-hour ride is uneventful as they coordinate with each other by two-way radio.

The *Gupka* is standing by to carry away the crew from the scuttled boats. They watch aboard the *Gupka* as their boats sink into the waters of the lake. Lake Erie is deep on its eastern end. The mission is almost complete. The *Gupka* raises its anchor and heads east to another zone. The morning is almost here as the ship has sailed through the night. It is 8:00 AM the next day. All parties are debarking at an unloading point in a New York port.

Two awaiting vans take the cell members to another parking lot where they pick up their leased cars for a ride away from the city. A house trailer has been rented and is parked at a camp in the mountains. All of the terrorists will rest at this remote camp. This backup plan is being used so things can cool down for a time. America might be a little too hot right now. Mr. Big is totally overjoyed by the mission. He says, "Maybe we can fry some bigger fish the next time. Perch town Fairport Harbor won't be the same for a while."

My body feels the aftershock of a night of heavy drinking. I'm talking to myself. "I started drinking yesterday before noon. I have to stop that. It was about 7:30 PM in the evening that I must have passed out. There was a news flash on TV about an explosion in Grand River, or was it a marsh fire?" I'm wondering to myself if I'm alive. "Was I at the Mardi Gras last night? Do I have any holes in my body? Am I even here? God help free me from this monster. I have again boozed myself into a *nightmare of terror*." I'm so mad at myself. I missed the fireworks again. I see the bottle of half-filled vodka. It's on the floor by my bed. I'm so ashamed. Alcohol is again leaving me shell shocked. I walk outside my front door as an ambulance roars by. Then another goes by and it is slowing down. Then I see a military jeep and an army personnel truck. There are police streaming into town. "What the hell?"

CHAPTER 27

❀

After the Attack

County sheriffs and the FBI secure an area around a burned out truck. The passengers and driver have been dissected by the explosion of a bomb placed under the truck seat. Little bits of evidence are picked up for analysis. Some of the weaponry used in the attack of Grand River village, Fairport Harbor, and the Perry power plant are recovered. Information gleaned from the scene is used to piece together some of the participants in this heinous operation. Help was needed to hide these terrorists. DNA samples of the corpses were sent to the national crime lab. A cell phone that was discovered near the crime scene still contained information about the perpetrators. Messages that were sent over cell phones provide clues to pinpoint the stores that were part of the terrorists' operation. Armed with this knowledge, a massive roundup of store owners and the staff was ordered by Homeland Security. Canadian authorities were welcomed into the fold to assist in determining their homeland involvement. This is an international investigation with far—reaching implications. FBI agents were joined by U.S. Marshals, local sheriff deputies and police from many communities. This was no ordinary get-the-bad-guy hunt. The terrorist lit an all engulfing fire that was consuming the nation's security blanket. A violation so devious underscored our vulnerability to be attacked. Locating the retreating enemy forces was a high priority.

The FBI knew the women were heading east. Traffic to Canada was halted for twenty-four hours at Niagara Falls. Vehicle inspections are taking place all over Pennsylvania and New York. A southern command post was established in Chardon, Ohio. This massive dragnet was ordered by Homeland Security as the nation went to high alert Code Red. *As the days passed, more information was gathered from the roundup in Lake County. The operation was cleverly disguised by using the food stores to hide the outlaws.*

A couple tips received by the FBI indicate a group of sailors were off loaded in Buffalo. Rented cars took off from a used car dealership in Buffalo. The trail was cold for awhile. Then national TV gave a description of cars that could be carrying the people wanted for questioning. A sighting in the Appalachian Mountains helped the police zero in on a campsite. SWAT teams made a raid of the hunting trailer and found the occupants had slipped away. The fast exit meant police were on the right trail. It appears they made the escape by switching to small aircraft. The rental cars found at an old runway matched the cars from a Buffalo car dealership.

The FBI was only a step away from catching the big fish. Lake County was being invaded with terrorists. The headlines in Ohio newspapers and across the nation detailed the terrorist travel pattern, the plan, and the Canadian involvement. All points, all citizens, be alert for unusual activity. The terrorist are invading from the north.

I was admitted to the hospital and strapped down for two days. Alcohol poisoning had caused me to collapse outside my home.

Doctor Pari said, "Richard, two FBI agents had visited you while you were detoxifying. They asked if they could talk with you. I gave them permission but you were delirious. Interesting though, the nurse said they stayed with you." The nurse added, "Agent Roman said they may need to talk with you again."

Dr. Pari said to me, "A huge terrorist ring has been broken in Lake County, Ohio. They rounded up a big guy and his associates. Yachts were confiscated and stores were being raided. All of this is going on and here you are in an alcoholic semi-coma. You missed it all," he said. "The FBI agents said they think you told them some important news. I told them, you're just dreaming."

"Fairport Harbor, Grand River, and Painesville are making national news. All of these terrorist were arrested right in these towns." He added, "I can't see how you could help the FBI in your state of mind."

I ask, "Dr. Pari, what date is it?"

"Richard, you've been out for a while. It's July 4th, Independence Day."

The End.

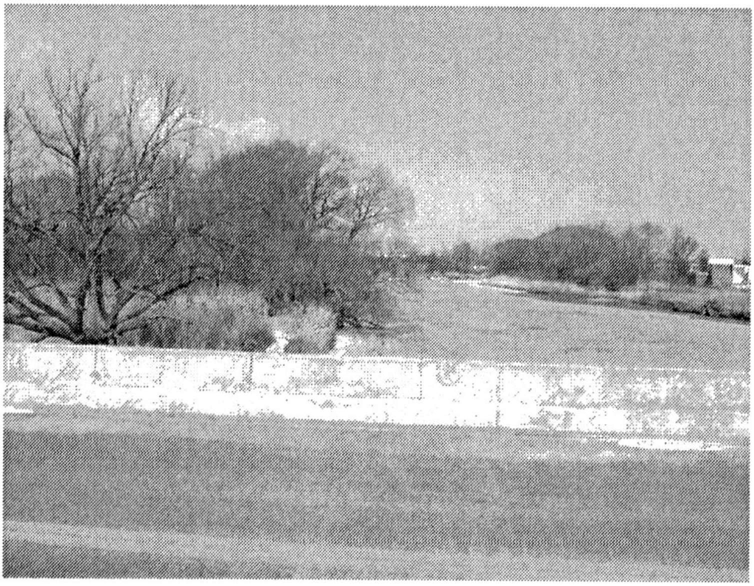

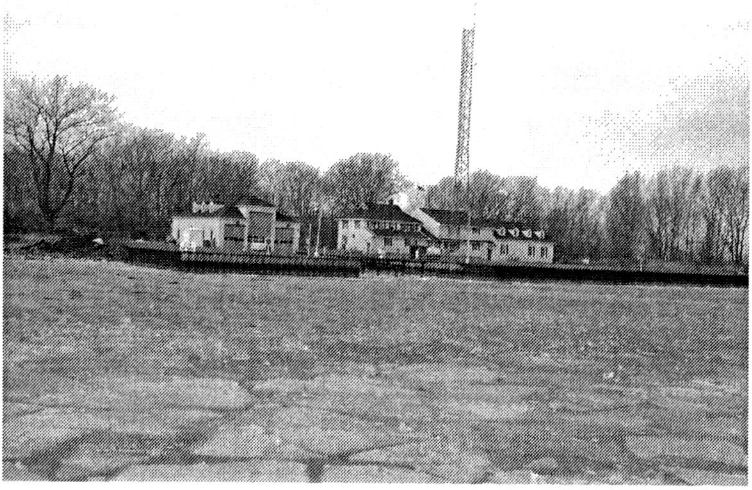

124   Terror by Invasion

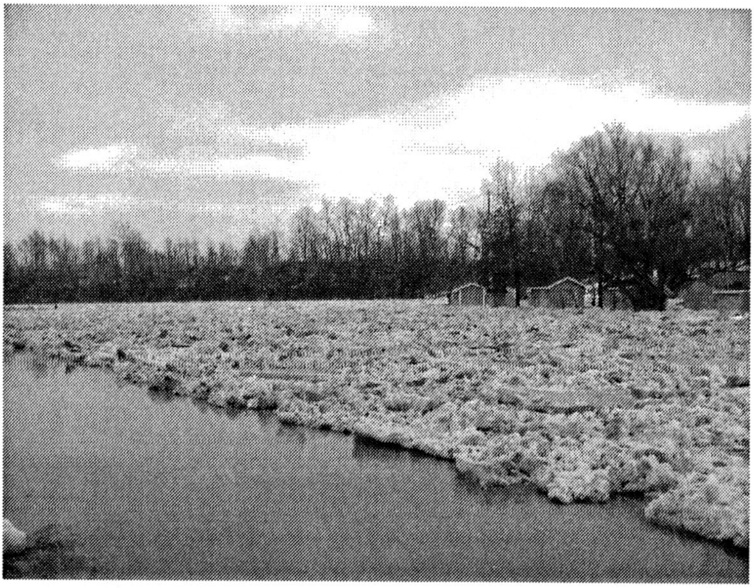

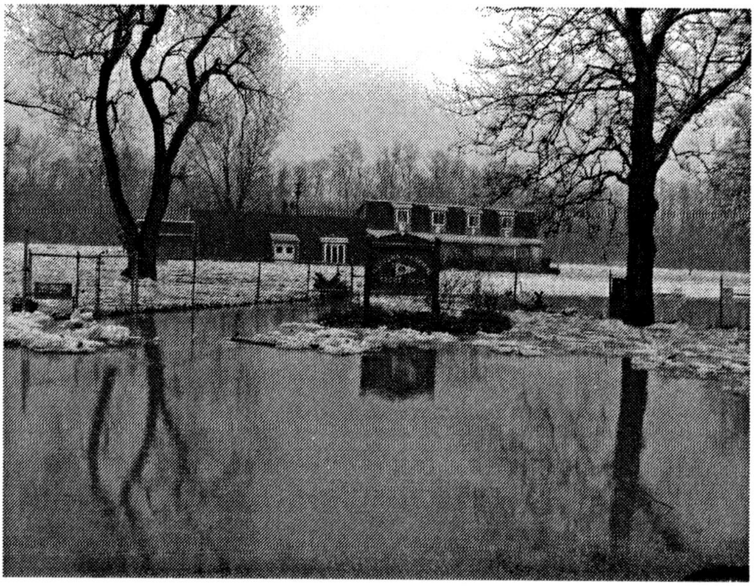

978-0-595-38468-6
0-595-38468-4